STICKY FINGERS

— LARGE PRINT EDITION —

JT LAWRENCE

FIRE FINCH

ALSO BY JT LAWRENCE

FICTION

SCI-FI THRILLER

WHEN TOMORROW CALLS

• SERIES •

The Stepford Florist: A Novelette

The Sigma Surrogate (prequel)

1. Why You Were Taken

2. How We Found You

3. What Have We Done

When Tomorrow Calls Box Set: Books 1 - 3

URBAN FANTASY

BLOOD MAGIC SERIES

1. The HighFire Crown
2. The Dream Drinker
3. The Witch Hunter
4. The Ember Isles
5. The Chaos Jar
6. The New Dawn Throne

STANDALONE NOVELS

The Memory of Water

Grey Magic

EverDark

SHORT STORY COLLECTIONS

Sticky Fingers

Sticky Fingers 2

Sticky Fingers 3

Sticky Fingers 4

Sticky Fingers: 36 Deliciously Twisted Short Stories: The
Complete Box Set Collection (Books 1 - 3)

NON-FICTION

The Underachieving Ovary

ABOUT THE AUTHOR

JT Lawrence is a bestselling author and playwright. She lives in Parkview, Johannesburg, in a house with a red front door.

Be notified of giveaways, special deals & new releases
by signing up to JT's mailing list.

www.jt-lawrence.com

facebook.com/JanitaTLawrence

twitter.com/pulpbooks

amazon.com/author/jtlawrence

bookbub.com/profile/jt-lawrence

*This book is dedicated to Julia-Ann Malone,
my Patron Saint of Short Stories*

STICKY FINGERS

VOLUME 1

CONTENTS

1

BRIDGE GATE

Dear Dad

Mom said it would be okay to write you a letter. I asked her when I'd see you again and she said she wasn't sure. I said I wanted to phone you but she said you're not taking calls at the moment. She said you might not answer the letter, either, but that I could try.

The address is to 'Bridge Gate' but I don't know what that is. It sounds like some kind of B&B. Are you staying at a B&B?

The problem with a letter is that I don't really know what to write. If we could talk then I think I would know what to say but a letter is different. It's like talking to an empty room.

Mom said to tell you about school. School is fine. I like English but I hate geography. In English we are reading some Shakespeare and it's difficult to understand but I like it anyway, especially Macbeth. Next year we will study Romeo & Juliet which I am looking forward to.

Me and Sarah-Jayne (she is my best friend) cut off all our hair the other day! Mom was cross but I think it's my hair and I can do what I want with it? I'm 11 now so it's not like I'm a little kid anymore. Anyway it didn't look THAT nice so S-J's mom took us to her hairdresser to tidy it up and it looks better now. Mom was happy. S-J's mom says I am a bad influence on S-J but Mom says it's the other way around. That's mother's for you! The hairdresser said I look more cheeky elvin now than keemo chic but I don't know what that means. I don't know what elvin or keemo is.

I'm going to stop writing and post this letter now. I hope you get it. I hope you reply. It's weird knowing that you have a dad out there somewhere but you don't get to see him. It's a little bit like you died.

Please write back!

Love from Em.

Dear Emily

I have included the letter that you sent me in this envelope. You will see I have made corrections where your spelling or grammar was incorrect. I hope you will study it thoroughly. Specifically I would like to point out your usage of "me and Sarah-Jayne" where it should have been "Sarah-Jayne and I". Also remember that contractions are signalled with apostrophes but plurals are not. Instead of writing "That's mother's for you" with an apostrophe, it should have been "mothers" (plural), without the apostrophe. Also, you use too many exclamation marks. Like insults, exclamation marks shouldn't be employed unless they are absolutely necessary.

By "elvin" I assume you meant "elfin" which means like an elf.

By "keemo" I assume you meant "chemo" as in "chemotherapy" which is a cancer treatment that can make your hair fall out (and is not to be made light of, especially by a hairdresser).

I hope this is clear.

Sincerely,

Your Father.

~

Dear Dad

I was so happy to get your letter, thank you!! I read the corrections you made and I will try not to make the same mistakes again. I like your red pen. Where did you get it? I have one that is similar but it is pink and it smells nice and when you shake it the glitter inside sparkles.

Sarah-Jayne and I had a fight about who is a better dancer (between us) but we are friends again. Her mom was so happy when we weren't speaking to each other and now she's not because we ARE speaking to each other again!. We're back to being best friends. S-J's mother pulls a funny face now when I'm over there. Like an old dog without teeth who tries to smile but can't. It's better to be at our house, anyway!. Mom's always at work so we get to do whatever we want. We watch American Idols and eat popcorn or cereal for dinner. Grilled cheese if we feel like cooking. There's not always that much food in the fridge but there is always cheese and bread.

What do you have for dinner there, where you are staying?

Love from Em.

PS. Sorry about all the crossing out. I keep using exclamation marks and then I remember what you said about them and then I take them out.

Dear Emily

I have again included your most recent letter to me, in this envelope. I see your spelling is improving. Your sentence structure can do with some work. You should not write "and then and then and then" but instead use the correct punctuation and conjunctions. In this instance, I would recommend thus: "I keep using exclamation marks, but then remember what you said about them, and take them out."

This is the written word, which should be clear and eloquent; not some reality TV marathon dance-off that leaves you out of breath.

Dinner this evening was pork sausages and mashed potato. There were some peas, too, but they were grey and best left alone.

Sincerely,

Your Father

~

Dear Dad

I can't remember the last time we had bangers and

mash! Yum! You're lucky. I miss mom's cooking. I don't remember your cooking. Did you ever cook? Maybe you were the best cook ever but I was too small to realise. Or it was too long ago to remember. Anyway, I know that Mom has to work all the time to keep the wolf away. At least she's still living in the house, kind of. I mean she's not home most of the time but when she is, it feels like she is far away. Like she's here, but she's not really here. Like she thinks herself into another room, or another house.

Sarah-Jayne's mother is worse than ever. S-J's father went away for a while (like you) but then he came back again. According to S-J's mother he's a loser and a Miss Cree-ant. No idea what a Miss Cree-ant is but she let him move back in and now she walks around all dog-face again.

I wish you'd come back. When I ask Mom if it will ever happen she just gives me the Death Stare. The Death Stare is when you look at someone with evil eyes and a cross face until they get the message that whatever they have done is NOT O.K.

I'm turning 12 on Saturday which means I'm almost a grown up. Mom wants to have a party at our house but I said that parties are for babies and that I just want to go ice-skating with S-J and Murray and then go for waffles afterwards at Milky Lane.

Do you ever go ice-skating at the B&B?

Love from Em

Dear Emily

Please find your most recent letter enclosed as usual.

A miscreant is a reprobate, a rogue, a rascal.

The saying is "to keep the wolf from the door" not "to keep the wolf away."

Your sentence structure is much improved, but I'm afraid your spelling has taken a turn for the worse. Perhaps a dictionary would come in handy? I used to have one in my office at home but I am assuming that my office is no longer. Perhaps your mother will know where it is. Ask her if you like; if you are not too afraid of getting another Death Stare.

We don't have waffles or ice-skating here. I miss neither.

Who is Murray?

Sincerely,

Father

Dear Dad

I asked Mom for your dictionary but she just stormed out of the room as if I said something wrong. She says I have an attitude problem but really I think she's the one with anger management issues. Anger management is when you get really really cross but then you just swallow it until later and then get it out in a constructive way like kick-boxing or pigeon shooting or something like that. She says ever since I turned 13 I've been a 'nightmare.' I didn't think that was a very nice thing to say.

Murray and Sarah-Jayne and I are best friends now. We do everything together. S-J borrows me nail polish and earrings (did I tell you I got my ears pierced?) and Murray borrows me books. Really interesting books that open my mind.

Anyway I looked everywhere for your dictionary and I found some pictures of you and mom when you were younger. I didn't know you were ever so happy. It felt weird to look at them — they made me happy and sad at the same time. I didn't say anything to Mom. I don't like to see her cry, even when she's being mean. I can't help thinking that you went away because of me.

What is it like where you are, Dad? What do you do all day at the B&B? It's hard to picture you there because I don't know anything about it.

Love from Em

Dear Emily

Recent letter enclosed. Please study it carefully. The correct way to use the term 'borrow' is 'lend to, borrow from,' and not the other way around. In other words, Sarah-Jayne lends you her nail polish and Murray lends you his books. You borrow nail polish and books from your friends.

Look again for the dictionary. It must be there somewhere.

What do I do here? I study and garden and try to stay alive. That's about it.

Sincerely,

Father

PS. I didn't leave because of you.

Dear Dad

I'm in love with Murray. I can't stop thinking about him and I spend geography class writing my name and his surname as if we were married. I think up names for the babies we will have one day. I know I'm only 14 but I wish we could get married. If we lived in Romeo and Juliet's time then we would be able to. My English teacher said so.

I was looking for your dictionary AGAIN the other day (it's just something I do sometimes when I wander around the house) and Mom just exploded (clearly her anger management is not going very well) and admitted that she packed up most of your things after you moved away and donated them to Hospice. I couldn't believe it! I hope you are not too upset. I have chosen a few of your things (what is left of your things, anyway) and have hidden them away in my bedroom so that she can't give those away, too. I know that she snoops through my things though so I can't promise I'll keep them forever.

What kind of gardening do you do at the B&B?

Love from Em

Dear Emily

You use too many parentheses in your writing. It's a bad habit. Try to stop it now before it's too late.

Don't be too hard on your mom. I'm sure she's trying her best. It's not easy for her.

I am in the middle of planting out a rose garden. It involves a great deal of digging and my hands are almost always lacerated by the thorns. They would sting in the shower if we ever got hot water here. The Bridge Gate is not a B&B.

Regarding Romeo & Juliet: try not to rush into anything. Keep in mind how that particular story turns out. We have a Shakespearean story (of sorts) playing out here. Instead of the Montagues and the Capulets, however, we have the BlackJacks and the White Collars. Although I disapprove of the division and don't want to be involved, I am seen as a White Collar. I try to mind my own business and tend to the important things, like the roses. In my experience nothing ever good comes from choosing sides.

Don't worry about my things. I have everything I need here. Keep what you want for yourself and throw the rest away.

Smith always says that the more possessions you have, the less energy you have because owning material things costs you energy. Less is almost always more. Sometimes I think Smith is full of it — he reads too much — but I think this is true, even though Smith collects bananas and keeps them under his pillow. For some reason he doesn't think the rule applies to bananas.

Sincerely,

Your Father

∿

Dear Dad

I hate Murray and Sarah-Jayne. Do you see these watermarks on the page? They are tears. My heart is in a million pieces. I tried to talk to Mom but all she says is 'good riddance' as if she doesn't care about my broken heart at all. I hate her. And I hate Sarah-Jayne. I wish I could hate Murray but when I think about him my chest just crumples inside. I need you, Dad. Can you please come and visit? You can sleep in my room and I will sleep in the lounge on the lumpy couch. I don't care.

Love from Em

PS. What are parentheses??

Dear Emily

Youth is full of excitement and heartache, and you should ride the waves while you can. At least that is what Perkins says. He is a philosopher, so he is probably right. On the other hand, sometimes he sings *La Traviata* (Italian opera) at the top of his voice and forgets to wear his pants, so perhaps we should take what he says with a pinch of salt.

There weren't any errors in your previous letter. 'Parentheses' are commonly known as 'brackets.'

I'm sorry I can't visit you. The rose garden is at its most vulnerable and needs daily attention.

Sincerely,

Father

Dear Dad

Mom is acting weird. I'm the one with the broken heart so you'd think that I'd be the one eating an entire litre of tin roof ice-cream in the lounge with the curtains drawn and watching *Come Dine With Me* reruns, but she has been hogging it instead. Sometimes when I get home from school she is just sitting there, and the phone is ringing. She acts as if she doesn't hear it. I know I was always complaining about her never being home but this is worse.

I don't like being at home anymore, but I don't like school either. Murray is there. I hate Murray. He is an asshole.

If you can't visit me here, maybe I can come visit you there at the B&B? I'd love to see the roses.

Love from Em

Dear Emily

Please refrain from using curse words in your letters to me and your writing in general. Curse words are for commoners and for people who lack a good vocabulary. Nothing good comes of swearing. It's a filthy habit, like smoking.

That said, if you must use the term 'asshole' please spell it correctly. We are not referring to a donkey. Hence: "arsehole" is the correct spelling.

I am not allowed visitors. Bridge Gate is not a B&B. Even if you were to come, the rose garden isn't blooming yet. You'd be disappointed.

Sincerely,

Your Father

Dear Dad

I can't believe Mom told you about the smoking! It was just once, and getting caught was just bad luck. It's not like I'm addicted or anything. The teacher that suspended me has never liked me and was SO happy to catch me doing something wrong. It didn't mean anything. I was just doing it to get back at Murray. He and S-J go around like life is so bloody wonderful (when it's NOT) and so when Vince asked me if I wanted to go share a cigarette with him in the boys' locker room (Vince always wears black and he listens to cool music and talks about deep stuff that I don't understand) of course I said YES.

Please don't be cross with me. Everyone else is cross enough.

Love from Em

Dear Emily

At least you spelt 'bloody' correctly.

Smith (he was talking about us, not about you) says that saints are just sinners who keep trying. I think it's true. So I'll keep trying, and you must, too.

One cigarette is not the end of the world. It's the boy you should be cautious of. Don't let your broken heart lead you down a barbed path you can't reverse out of. Murray is not worth it, and

Sarah-Jayne is certainly not worth it. Besides, the best revenge is to be successful. You won't be successful if you keep skipping class to smoke with a boy, no matter how interesting he is.

Perkins says that our poor life choices are like tattoos — you can try to get rid of them but they'll always be there, under the skin. Best not to get a tattoo in the first place.

Sincerely,

Your Father

Dear Dad

Okay, okay, I won't get the tattoo. How did you know about it, anyway? Mom swears she hasn't spoken to you in years so I don't know where you're getting your intel from. 'Intel' means intelligence, as in information. I learnt it from the TV. I've been watching a lot of TV lately because what else am I supposed to do when I'm suspended from school? Mom has forbidden me from seeing Vince. I think everyone is overreacting. (Although I am glad that Mom is off the couch and in the land of the living again, even if it is just to shout at me).

Thank God that I'll be 16 soon. 16 is pretty much an adult. Sweet 16! Ha! More like the opposite. I don't want a party if you can't come. Maybe I can write a letter to someone there and ask nicely to let you come out just for a weekend? I am getting good at writing letters!

Love from Em

Dear Emily

I'm afraid a letter from you, no matter how well-written it is, will not secure an exit pass for me for the weekend. Besides, things are very busy here and I can't leave Smith. He has a cracked skull and some broken ribs. He was in the hospital wing for a few days but now he's back and I need to look after him. He is not to be left alone.

Sincerely,

Your Father.

~~Holy Shit~~ Dad

What happened to Smith??

Em

Dear Emily

There is no need to use two question marks after your questions. One will suffice.

Smith got himself into a spot of bother with another resident. A BlackJack, as you have probably guessed. Next time he will know better. We live and learn, as Pant-less Perkins says.

Sincerely,

Your Father

Dear Dad

Did they get into a fight? What were they fighting about?

I got into a fight with S-J last week (who else?!) but there were no broken ribs exchanged, just horrible words.

I have always pictured Smith as a respectable accountant type of person. Not someone who gets into fights! Perkins, too. Are they not?

I am secretly dating Vince now, despite (or maybe because of) everyone's pressure not to. I don't know why people think they can just tell me what to do as if I'm some kind of sheep. Mom bought me some colourful tops the other day because she's tired of me wearing black all the time and because she felt bad that we are always fighting. If she could stop telling me what to do we'd probably get on better. I'm not some kid she can just boss around. She keeps searching my room for drugs but I told her I'm 16, not stupid. (The smokes she found were Vince's, not mine).

Love from Emily

Dear Emily

The altercation concerned a pack of cigarettes, I believe. Not dissimilar to your argument with your mother.

Smith is neither respectable nor an accountant. Perkins is even worse, but it's not his fault.

Despite their shortcomings, they have many redeeming qualities. Smith is kind and shares his paper with me so that I can write to you. Perkins … well, Perkins tries his best but he has had a difficult life.

We had bangers and mash for dinner this evening and it made me think of you. We also had carrots cut into coins that had all the goodness boiled out of them. A bit like Perkins.

Sincerely,

Your Father

Dear Dad

I need help. I feel like life is not worth living. I know it's a cliché but I don't care. I don't care about anything. Now I am the one sitting in the dark lounge and not talking to anybody. How do you get the goodness back into the carrot coins? There must be a way. I have given mine away and now I regret it. I feel used and soul-shrivelled. I need my carroty-ness back.

Love from Em

∼

Dear Emily

Your writing has come along so well. I am proud of you.

I'm afraid once the carroty-ness is gone it is gone forever. But don't despair. Your carroty-ness is not the only thing you have going for you. There are other parts of you that are in full bloom that you must be proud of.

Love, Dad.

∼

Dear Dad

You have no idea how your previous letter saved my life. Thank you. I love you.

Em

Dear Dad

I'm much better. I'm back in school. Vince is history. Mom and I are talking. My marks are improving.

I haven't heard from you in a while. How are the roses? Are you okay?

Love from Em

Dad

Are you okay??

Em

To my dearest Em

Smith has been killed. He was in another fight and a man named Axxe drove a shiv into his stomach. Talk about nominative determinism.

Nominative Determinism is when you live up to your name. For example, a plumber named Piper, or a chef named Cook. Perkins said my name would also make a good example, being Locklear, and being held here. You'd better not live up to your name. Maybe you SHOULD get married early after all, to a Bond or a Gold, or, even better: a Joy.

Try to forgive S-J and Murray, even if they don't deserve it. Hate is a destructive emotion: like drinking poison and expecting the other person to die.

When I found Smith in the library he was still alive but there was too much blood lost. We had a small ceremony yesterday where we all said a few words. It's not the same without him. No more stockpiled bananas, for one. Perkins (wearing pants, for a change) said that if he had to choose between feeling grief and feeling nothing, he'd take grief. I'm not too sure about that.

Someone from our side (a White Collar) witnessed the thing and Axxe has been thrown in solitary confinement. We won't tell them who the witness is, despite their threats. He did the right thing, and now we need to protect him. I don't want you to worry.

I am writing especially to let you know that the rose garden is flourishing. I also wanted to let you know that every rose I planted was for you. Every time I received a letter from you, I planted a new rose. There are 15 now and they look beautiful.

Don't be afraid of wearing some colour. There is a time for wearing black.

Tell your mom that I love her; that I never stopped loving her.

I never stopped loving you. I'm not a man for re-grets but I'll always be sorry for how things turned out between you and Mom and I.

The wonderful thing about having children is that

they can fix what you have broken. You are my up-grade, Em. Keep trying. Do better.

Love from Dad

Dear Dad

I found your dictionary!!! At last. And I'm coming to visit. Mom will bring me. She said she loves you, too. That's why it's so hard for her.

Love from Em

Dear Susan and Emily Locklear

It is with deep regret that I write to inform you of the passing away of your husband and father, Michael Locklear.

Mr Locklear was involved in an altercation. We don't believe there was much pain.

The men responsible have been transferred to the maximum security wing pending their trial, the details of which we will furnish in subsequent communication.

Mr Locklear was always a polite and generous man, and he transformed the gardens in the years he spent here. We are grateful for his work. In his studies, he completed various degrees and tutored others. His positive attitude and hard work are some of the qualities the parole board took into account when they granted his early parole yesterday, unaware of the fact that he had just passed away.

Please find the attached box of flowers that a fellow prisoner, Perkins, insisted you have. Inside is a bloom cut from each of the roses he had worked on every day for the past 6 years. My thoughts are with you in this difficult time.

With my sincerest condolences —

Frederick Collis

Director at Bridge Gate Prison

Department of Correctional Services

2

THE ITCH

I t starts as a tickle. A pin prickle. As if there is an insect on her scalp. It wakes her up. It isn't difficult to interrupt Sam's sleep. She hears everything at night: every serrated cat fight, every wail of house alarm, every empty midnight argument within a two block radius. It isn't a sudden alertness, like when a car backfires and sends her heart sprinting; sends her mind wandering into fantasies of hot guns and wasted bullets.

No. It's a slow surfacing; an un-rushed floating up from the warm depths of slumber. If she opened her eyes she would see the very first drafts of light spilling like smoke from behind the blinds.

Certain it's her imagination pulling at her follicles, Sam ignores the urge to swat away the phantom beetle. She tries to drift back down into the still murk but it has been disturbed; dredged from dark into colour.

One day, she says to herself, swinging her legs off the bed. One day I won't wake up exhausted.

One day you won't wake up at all, says a voice that sounds like her own.

At least, then, she says, I won't be exhausted.

Well, that's one way to look at it, says the voice. *Only you would think Death has a silver lining.*

Ha, says Sam.

What's wrong with you? the voice asks. *You used to be a pessimist.*

I don't have the energy to be a pessimist anymore.

She rubs her feet together, knits her fingers, stretches.

Is it normal, do you think, says Sam, to have conversations with yourself?

What do you mean, 'normal'?

Well, do other people do it?

Would that make it 'normal'? Anyway, why does it matter?

Sam sighs. She knows better than to get into a philosophical debate with herself so early in the morning. She yawns and knuckle-scrubs her swollen eyes. She thinks the itch is gone.

'You're early!' Pete from Accounting says.

Why does he always act surprised that you're early? says the voice. *Besides, he's always here before you, so that makes him even earlier.*

It's just something to say, that's all. He doesn't mean anything by it.

'Hi, Pete,' says Sam. 'Good weekend?'

'Yip, yip,' he says, 'Yip, it was a good one.'

She can tell by the way his eyes move upwards that he is searching for something interesting to say. Sam lifts her laptop bag as a signal that she should be working, and he gives up and lets her go. As she passes him she gets a faint whiff of wool and cologne. It smells wrong. Plain soap would suit him better.

She reaches her office and sighs down into her swivel chair. Switches on her machine. Starts her regular morning ritual of clearing her desktop of the previous day's chaos. Her stomach snarls.

Should have had breakfast, says the voice.

Yes, says Sam.

You had the time.

Yes.

Pete's rosy cheeks appear in her doorframe. He waits for her nod before crossing the threshold, and places a steaming cup of coffee on her desk with exaggerated care.

Ah, look, it's your favourite mug, says the voice.

'It's your favourite mug,' says Pete. 'Half a sugar, dash of milk.'

'You know me so well, Pete,' says Sam. 'You're a saint.'

'No,' blushes Pete.

'Saint Peter,' she smiles. He smiles back.

They crucified him upside-down, you know, says the voice. *Caesar's lot. That's really nothing to smile about.*

At her lunch hour (Emmentaler and ham on rye) Sam wonders if she should phone the boys; see what they're up to on their school holidays. She always has to weigh up the consequences of hearing Barry's disapproving tone, like ice water, versus the warm buoyancy she gets when she hears the animation in her sons' voices.

Bugger him, says the voice. *They're your kids too.*

I lost them, says Sam.

They're not lost, says the voice.

She's about to dial when there is another barely-there prickle on her scalp: a bright green caterpillar;

a fruit bug; a hornet. Her fingers fly up to inspect the spot: half expecting nothing; half expecting the shock of a small interloper. She scratches the vacant patch. There is temporary relief, but then it returns with double the intensity. She shoots up, sending the chair coasting backwards and crashing into the wall. She turns her head upside down and rubs her whole scalp frantically, trying to dislodge the itch.

What is it? asks the voice. *What is that feeling?*

Sam is too busy shaking her hair out to answer.

She's certain that if there ever was an insect, it's now gone, but the itch remains. She walks down the corridor to the restroom, where she parts her hair, leans over the basin, inspects the skin under the downlight.

There's nothing there, says the voice.

There must be something, says Sam. A mosquito bite. A hive. A blister.

There's nothing there.

It's itching like … like … I don't know, I've never had an itch as … ferocious as this before.

Don't scratch it.

I have to!

Don't scratch it! It's making it worse.

I don't care. I can't help it.

We need to get to a doctor.

A doctor? laughs Sam. It's an itch!

It could be something bad.

Oh please. Like what?

Shingles.

Shingles! I'm not an old man!

Your immune system is compromised.

No it is not! … Besides, shingles is more of a pain, isn't it? This is an itch.

It could be anything. Let's just pop in at the medical suites on our way home. See Doctor Callie.

Stop being such a hypochondriac.

Chicken pox!

It's not chicken pox. I had chicken pox when I was five. Still have the scars on my stomach where I could scratch without my mother seeing.

I know.

You know?

I was there.

I need to get back to work.

No you don't. You're days ahead. Take the rest of the day off. Maybe you just need some down time.

I can't just leave the office halfway through the day!

You used to.

That was another time. Another life. I'm not the same person.

Sam still finds herself shocked by how quickly an ordinary life can be derailed by just a couple of bad choices. She won't make the same mistakes again.

Stop scratching, Samantha, for God's sake.

I hate it when you call me 'Samantha.'

. . .

The parking lot is still full of cars when Sam reverses out. The security guard looks surprised that she is leaving early. She winds down her window.

'I'm just off to the doctor,' she says, to ease the guilty edges of her thoughts. Brown, foxed, like the pages of a well-read book. 'I'll be back soon.'

'Hope it's nothing serious,' the guard says.

She wants to say 'it's nothing' but then her excuse will be blown. She scratches her head.

'I'll be okay,' she says.

So we are *going to the doctor?* asks the voice.

May as well, says Sam. It's Monday afternoon and the sun is shining. What else do we have to do?

Doctor Callie surveys Sam's scalp.

'I can't see anything,' she says. Cheerful.

Is she blind? asks the voice.

What?

She just said she can't see anything.

She meant that she can't see anything *wrong*, says Sam. Anything *unusual.*

'I mean, it's a bit red, maybe from you scratching it?' says the doctor.

'I've been trying not to, but it's so … the itch is so intense.'

'Well,' she says, 'I can give you some topical steroids. That should help.'

We could have bought cortisone cream over the counter! What a waste of time.

You're the one who insisted we come here.

Do I hear a duck in here?

What?

Quack!

What else can she do? Sam asks the voice. She can't diagnose something she can't see.

Doctor Callie types the script up on an old school typewriter on her desk. Sam studies the antique.

'Yes,' she says, mid-type. 'I'm a walking cliché. My handwriting is *that* bad.'

Sam balls up her fists, denies the beckoning itch.

'It's extra strength. Schedule 4,' Callie says, pulling it out of the machine and handing it to Sam. 'Use it sparingly.'

Oh. Okay. Extra strength. That sounds good.

'Come back if any more symptoms develop.'

The bald pharmacist passes her the tube of ointment. Sam inspects his shiny scalp.

'Apply to the rash as needed,' he shouts for the whole pharmacy to hear.

Sam's cheeks flare.

'It's not a rash,' she says.

'Huh?' his eyebrows are like climbing ants.

'Never mind.'

It's not a venereal disease, she wants to tell everyone. It's not herpes or syphilis.

— As far as you know — says the voice.

It's not contagious, she wants to say.

As far as you know, says the voice.

Sam doesn't wait to get home before puncturing the tin tube and rubbing the ointment into the offending skin. She sits in her car, waiting for the relief. She taps her steering wheel.

Do you feel like driving somewhere? asks the voice.

Not particularly, says Sam. Unless you mean home. I would like to be at home.

I mean ... maybe the itch is psychosomatic.

It's not. The itch is real.

Psychosomatic doesn't mean it's not real. It means it's caused by your mind.

If it's caused by my mind then I should be able to stop it with my mind and believe me, I can't.

Have you tried?

Yes.

Try again.

Well, I've got the cream on now. The cream should work. How will I know if I cured myself with my amazing mental self-healing powers or if it was the cortisone?

Let's go home.

Yes. Let's.

Sam closes the front door behind her, hangs up her keys and her jacket. Sits on the creaking couch in her lounge holding the ointment in both hands like prayer beads. Kicks off her pumps, lies down with a throw pillow under her head and another under the backs of her knees. Comforting. The itch has definitely receded. She can still feel it nagging, but it seems further away. As if it's in the next room.

What shall we do now? asks the voice.

Why do you always want to *do* something?

What do you mean?

What is wrong with lying here?

Just lying here?

Yes. Just lying here for a moment. What is wrong with that?

It won't just be a moment. That's the thing. Besides, life is about doing things, isn't it? Doing one thing after another. A string of events. Lying on your couch is not an event.

I'm tired.

You're always tired.

You make me tired.

Maybe if you did something you wouldn't be as tired.

Maybe if you gave me a break I wouldn't be as tired.

Sam lies there for a while in the quiet cool of the room. There is no sound apart from the hum of the refrigerator and the occasional car passing outside. An hour passes in peace.

Sam waits for the voice to nag her, but it doesn't.

You know that things are bad, she thinks, when you give yourself the silent treatment.

. . .

It's itchy again, says Sam, but no one answers her. It's itchy! Damn it! Aren't you going to say something?

What do you want me to say? says the voice. *I thought you wanted me to keep quiet.*

Don't be petulant. It doesn't suit you.

Alright.

Alright?

Put some cream on. It definitely helped last time.

I have.

When?

Earlier, when you weren't talking to me.

Put some more on.

The doctor said to not use too much, says Sam.

She doesn't know how itchy it is.

True.

Desperate times call for desperate measures.

Yes. I'll put some more on.

Sam squeezes more ointment out, applies it liberally to the irritated patch.

There. You'll feel better now.

What if I don't?

Let's worry about that later.

I'm not going to be able to sleep tonight.

It won't be the first time.

True.

You'll live.

Yes, Sam sighs, yes, I suppose I will.

It's not working, says Sam. It's even worse than before.

Give it some time, says the voice.

I've given it time. I'm going to put some more on.

Are you sure?

It's just cream. What's the worst that can happen?

You shouldn't tempt fate.

I don't believe in fate.

Yes, you do.

You've been lying here for ages. Let's get up. Make some dinner.

There's nothing in the fridge.

Crackers, then. Cheese. I think there might be an old apple lurking in the fruit bowl. You have to eat something.

An old apple, says Sam. That sounds appealing.

She gets up slowly, rolls her head around on her neck. Finds a rind of cheddar but no crackers. No apple, old or otherwise. Puts on the kettle to have tea instead.

Maybe we can go grocery shopping tomorrow. Just to get a few things. You know, if you're feeling up to it.

. . .

Stop scratching!

What?

You're scratching like a rabid cat. Stop it.

Hey, I was sleeping!

Yes, well, maybe sleeping isn't such a great idea if it means you're going to scratch your head open.

I can't believe you woke me up. You know how difficult it is for me to —

Sam stops talking when she notices the sticky feeling on her fingers, the smell of copper. She switches on her bedside lamp. A bright halo jumps out of the bulb. Her fingers are bloody. Sam's confused. Where is the blood coming from?

I told you, says the voice.

Bright blood all over her pillow.

Oh my God.

Sam feels as though she has been attacked. As if a

man dressed in a black balaclava had come through the window and battered her.

Why does it always have to be a man? asks the voice.

What are you talking about?

Your imaginary intruder.

Because they almost always *are* men, says Sam. Men are the ones that harm. Mostly.

Have I ever hurt you? asks the voice.

No. I don't think so.

You don't think so?

No, you haven't. Now can we get back to this … massacre … on my pillow?

What is there to say?

It's still itchy, for one. Shall I put more steroid cream on?

Er, I don't think you realise —

What?

— How much damage you've done.

Sam gets out of bed, pads into the en suite. Gasps at the spectre in the mirror. Matted hair dyed red. As if perfectly choreographed, a fresh rivulet spills down her forehead.

Is this real? she asks. Is this really happening? It feels like a scene from a horror movie.

Stephen King, says the voice. *Carrie. The sad girl with magic powers. Pig's blood. Everyone dies in the end.*

You're not helping.

Sorry.

Sam leans forward to get a closer look. She is both repulsed and fascinated by the dark gash in her scalp.

Emergency room? says the voice.

At 3AM? It's not that bad.

It needs stitches.

No it doesn't. It needs a plaster. A shower and a plaster.

You can't be serious.

What do you know? demands Sam.

She turns on the hot water. Strips off her bloodied sleep shirt and kicks it towards the laundry bin. The steam billows, filling up the bathroom with its soothing mist. Sam steps into the smoky cube, tentatively moving her head underneath the rose. The water drums down on her lacerated scalp. It stings with a white light.

Sweet Jesus it stings!

Of course it bloody well stings, says the voice. *It's an open wound!*

Tinted water rushes down her body. She massages her hair, scrapes the dried blood from underneath her nails. The hot water hurts, but it takes away the itch. Pain. Relief. Pain. She stands there until the water runs clear and cold. Wraps herself up in a clean towel, shivers at her new reflection. Washed out. The only plasters she has in the house are five years old and have Mickey Mouse on them.

Why did I keep these? she asks herself, but there is no answer. She tears the paper off with her teeth. Uses three to cover the abraded area. Cuts her nails as short as they will go. Puts on some warm clothes. Casual. She won't be going in to work today, not with Disney plasters on her head.

Sam sits on the chair in the dawn-dark bedroom, waiting for the day to begin.

You could try to sleep, says the voice.

Ha, says Sam. Sometimes it's like you don't know me at all.

Ha, says the voice.

Sam waits. She taps her toes. Sighs.

Still itchy.

Yes.

That's surprising. I would have thought you had scratched all the nerve endings to death.

I wish I had.

This isn't healthy. Sitting here in the gloom.

Let me guess. You want to do something.

You don't actually have to do *something. You just need a* distraction. *You could just put something on. The TV. Read a book.*

That's a good idea, she says, but she doesn't move.

I know what you're thinking, says the voice. *Stop. Just stop. You're just making it harder.*

I can't help it.

Yes, you can. You know how.

I'm too tired. That's the problem. Worn down. How can I hang on to willpower when I feel this way?

You'll feel better soon. You just need to get through this ... whatever this is.

I need a drink.

Don't say it! Don't even say the words.

I can't help it. The thought just comes again and again like a ... stubborn boomerang. It's like a sick mantra that won't go away. I need a drink I need a drink I need a drink.

Please. Stop.

You know I won't do it. I won't. But I can't help the urge. What's the point in denying it exists? It's always there. Every time I walk past that kitchen cupboard. Every time I open that drawer in the study. My shoe cupboard. The vanity desk. Every single time I crave that glass bottle lip in my mouth.

... I know.

When will it end?

I don't know.

'Good gracious, Miss Douglas, what have you done to yourself?'

Sam blushes as the doctor peels away the cartoon characters.

'I'm usually such a bad sleeper. I can't believe I did so much damage in my sleep.'

'Your inhibitions are lower when you're asleep. You didn't have anyone to tell you not to scratch.'

Sam chokes on air.

'You tried the cortisone?'

'Yes.'

'It didn't help?'

'I thought it was helping. And then I woke up with blood all over my pillow.'

The doctor cleans the wound and applies a fresh dressing. She keeps it in place by winding a bandage all the way around Sam's head, tucking it under her chin.

'I look like a wounded soldier or something. All I need now is a limp and a wooden crutch.'

'At least you can laugh about it,' the doctor says, reeling more and more gauze around Sam's head.

'Is all the bandaging really necessary?'

'It's to stop you from scratching it open again tonight.'

Okay. That makes sense.

'This time we'll give you a full blood work-up. Try to figure out what's causing it. And I'm going to give you oral cortisone. Whether the pills help or not, I'd like you to see a specialist.'

'A dermatologist?' asks Sam. 'That's a good idea.'

Why didn't I think of that?

'A psychiatrist,' says Callie, sitting down at her typewriter. Rolling up her sleeves. 'I'll give you a list of my recommendations in the area.'

'I already have one,' says Sam. 'A psychologist.'

'Oh?' says Callie, mid-clack.

'A counsellor,' says Sam. 'I'm an alcoholic.'

'You didn't tell me that,' says the doctor.

'It was an itch. I didn't think it was relevant,' says Sam.

'In this kind of case, everything is relevant.'

This time Sam is not woken by blood. Her bed linen is wet again, but it's not crimson, like before. It's clear, tinged with pink and green.

You've scratched right through that ridiculous dressing, says the voice.

Oh, God, says Sam. Why didn't you wake me?

I did!

Why did I go to sleep in the first place? I should have just stayed awake. What is this liquid? Is the wound weeping? Is it infected?

This time I really think you should go to the ER. I know it's the middle of the night but —

Okay. I think I will.

The intern on duty clicks his penlight torch and peers at Sam's head. Startles. Shines it into her eyes. He grabs a gurney for her, books an operating room and darts her with an IV.

That escalated quickly, says Sam.

The voice is quiet. Is it still a voice if it is quiet? she wonders.

It looks pretty serious, prods Sam.

There is excited babbling around her.

... They're just being careful. Better safe than sorry, says the voice.

I should probably call the boys.

There's no time.

They rush her under fluorescent lighting that leaves trails in her vision. A long exposure gone wrong till the picture is ruined. Bleached. Blown out. An oxygen mask is strapped to her face. Someone holds her cold hand. Anaesthetic pulls her under; her whole body is dunked by the drugs and the relief.

'Samantha?' says a white lab coat. 'Samantha? Can you hear me?'

Sam groans. Opens her eyes. Her mouth is stuck together. Her head feels like it has exploded. She lifts her hand to touch it but there is only a cocoon of dry bandaging. She tries to swallow the cotton-mouth but her swallow-reflex is on strike.

'Waa rara?' asks Sam.

'What happened?' says the lab coat. 'You managed to scratch through —

Scratched through my scalp? says Sam. That's terrible.

'You scratched through your skull.'

That's not even possible. That's not possible, is it?

'It was brain fluid. You actually scratched into your brain.'

Sam can't tell if he is horrified or fascinated. He tells her that while she was out, a neurosurgeon had cleaned and debrided the site, which had become infected. A plastic surgeon had grafted perforated ribbons of her thigh skin over it.

'Thank you,' she says. What else could she say?

'Did you count things as a child?' asks the hospital psychiatrist, pen hovering over chipped clipboard.

Of course I counted things as a child. It was called school.

Sam nods. Her head pounds.

'I mean, count things compulsively,' says the psychiatrist.

'No,' says Sam.

'Did you skip over cracks in the pavement, that kind of thing?'

'No,' says Sam. 'I'm not obsessive-compulsive.'

'OCD would explain this ... situation.'

'I'm not saying it's *not* psychological,' says Sam, 'just that I'm not OCD.'

The psychiatrist purses his lips; not convinced. Sam knows she is inconveniencing him.

The itch remains: furious and all-consuming. A modest flower arrangement arrives: yellow tulips from Pete from Accounting. "Get Well Soon!" the card says.

I don't understand, says Sam.

You don't understand why Pete would send you flowers?

I don't understand why it's still itchy. I mean, it's not even the same skin. It's from my leg.

You're right. It doesn't make any sense.

It's like my actual brain is itchy. I can't stand it. When it's at it's worst, I fantasise …

Yes?

I fantasise about getting a steel brush and just scrubbing away.

Instead, she lies on her side, hands clenched, and watches the tulips fade.

'Hi,' says a new lab coat. Freshly washed hair, red lipstick, happy clinking gold bangles. Sam envies the doctor's non-itchy scalp. Wonders if she has any of her own hair left under the swathes of gauze. She imagines herself looking like a giant human cotton bud.

'Don't worry,' the red lipstick says. 'I don't think you're crazy.'

'Then you don't know me very well,' says Sam. It hurts to smile.

She seems nice, says the voice.

The neurologist injects local anaesthetic into Sam's scalp. It helps for a few glorious hours, and then the itch comes back. They continue this treatment in waves of itch and relief and itch and relief until the medicine stops working.

Sam wakes up to find that despite the dressings she has rubbed away the skin graft. She is returned to the operating room for a new one. She rubs that one away, too. She is declared a danger to herself and is transferred to a psychiatric institution where they tie her hands to the bedposts at night to stop her from scratching.

We have to get out of here! says the voice.

I don't know. It's not that bad, says Sam.

Not that bad? It's a nut house! You're not mentally ill!

I know.

But?

But it's nice to be taken care of. It's nice to be able to sleep. It's been a long time. I feel better.

One day the man who shares the room with her is gone. He was friendly and always wore quirky socks. Dots and stripes and jolly colours. Liquorice Allsorts. He shared his fruit baskets with her.

There's hope, she tells the voice. *See? Mr P has been discharged.*

He, too, suffered from a persistent itch and had his hands wrapped up in white. The two were like boxers, the nurses would joke as they performed the evening ritual. Sparring partners. Except that instead of fighting they would sit and have tea together and complain about the early lights-out.

Sam knows that Mr P was not, in fact, cured. She saw the stained sheets, the congealed brown puddle on the floor. The sisters' shiny swollen eyelids. Mr P's itch had been on his neck, over his carotid artery.

A dangerous place to scratch, whispers the voice.

. . .

I wonder if the boys will visit, says Sam.

I'm sure they will, says the voice.

Sam is discharged once the staff formulate a way to stop her from hurting herself. She is given a soft helmet to wear at night, and cotton mitts. At its worst the itch is as violent as ever, but Sam protects herself. If she really has to scratch she uses the toddler's toothbrush she hadn't been able to throw away all those years ago. A lifetime ago. She wakes up to the solace of a clean pillow every morning. Her hair grows back in unattractive tufts. She walks with a slight gait: minor cerebrum damage from when she scratched her brain. She plans to return to work. She plans to call the boys and laugh with them on the phone. She plans to go for coffee with Pete from Accounting.

A neighbour's house alarm is howling. It's 4AM. Sam feels surrounded by the night. Her scalp itches.

It's good that you're taking advantage of your situation, says the voice.

My situation? says Sam.

Yes. You're home. You're alive. You're sober. You've got a job. You can walk.

Yes, says Sam, reaching for the toothbrush. She re-moves the helmet and moves the soft bristles in slow circles over the itch. Sighs at the intense and sweeping relief.

You're lucky, says the voice.

I wouldn't go that far.

You still have a sense of humour.

Do I? asks Sam.

I don't know, says the voice. *What do I know?*

Sam stretches, swings her legs out of bed. Thinks of Mr. P's candy coloured socks.

Maybe … starts Sam.

Yes? says the voice.

Maybe we can do something today.

~

3

THE UNSUSPECTING GOLD DIGGER

W hen I first slept with Byron I didn't know about the money. I don't think anyone did.

They weren't handing out silver spoons the days we were born. His parents were decidedly middle-class, as were mine, and while we didn't want for much, we were by no stretch of the imagination Trust Fund Kids. We weren't in line to inherit much either, once our folks eventually decided to leap off their respective mortal coils, which looked as if it would be further and further into the future the way they were soldiering on, making them-selves raw green juices for breakfast and embracing meditation and tai chi. It's not like I wished them dead — far from it — but I did wonder from time to time how old they would allow themselves to get. It's about being practical: I mean, old age isn't pretty. Letting yourself get any older than 90, I think, isn't respectable. There are plenty of ways you can stop this from happening: it doesn't have to be gruesome. In fact, the whole point is to avoid vulgarity altogether.

Byron and I both went to good government schools in Johannesburg. We had nice clothes but not the best, good sporting equipment but not the most expensive. We grew up middle-of-the-road and although we only met when we were in our mid-30s, we could have easily have known each other for years, because he was exactly like my brothers and the other boys I knew, and I, like his sister. We knew the same jokes and had the same boarding school horror-food stories, which we would still exchange in new company 20 years on. In moments like these it was easy to feel as if we had known each other our whole lives. There was an inherent intimacy in our relationship, something sharp and soft at the same time, embedded deep in our connection with each other. An oyster at the bottom of our ocean.

We met online — not on a dating site, but a travel forum — and our relationship developed quickly. There was no playing hard to get on either side: there was no need. We both saw what we wanted and both got lucky. When you're on your way downhill from 35 and you manage to link arms with a fellow slider who you find reasonably attractive and who makes you laugh you don't think twice about 'moving too fast'. We were comfortable with each other from the beginning; mature enough to be able to just be ourselves. We had similar interests, and a shared love of modern literature, red wine, and any movie starring Will Ferrell. We kind of slid into each other's lives; slid into each other. We ate from each others' plates, split our paperbacks and shared our socks. We kissed before brushing our teeth.

The first warning bell was the size of the diamond he gave me. No, that's not right. The actual warning bell was the diamond itself, and what it represented. The size just magnified the alarm. We had spoken about marriage fleetingly — Byron knew that it wasn't an institution I was particularly fond of — and I had thought that there was no need to mention it again.

I didn't believe in committing to one person for the rest of one's life. At the rate people change, I didn't find it practical.

Our relationship was evermore altered on a humid April morning on Reunion Island. Byron had insisted on waking up early and taking a walk to the beach while it was still empty. I wanted to lie in, doze, and finish the book I was reading. He made bourbon vanilla tea and threw pillows at me, bribing me with how lovely the dawn view would be. I told him to go on his own. He promised a cappuccino and *pain au chocolate* on the walk down, and I acquiesced. Coffee and pastry in hand, gazing at the last of the sunrise, we sat on the still-cool sand while the air around us swirled with something yet unfamiliar to us. There was a peculiar tension, an odd anxiety that I couldn't understand. I brushed it off, thinking I was just out of sorts because of the early rise, but it kept returning, nagging at my mood, like a pebble in a shoe.

"I have something for you," he finally said, breaking the spell of awkwardness.

Thank God, I thought. The unease was just about a small gift that he was hiding, figuring out how to give it to me. Secrecy was the thing making us uncomfortable — we weren't accustomed to it. I looked at his empty hands, then searched his lit-up eyes for clues.

"I'm not sure you'll like it."

"Well, that's a good start," I joked. He laughed out of nervousness, not at my wit. The pebble was back. Before I could make another attempt at banter he reached into his board-shorts pocket and brought out a small black box hinged with gold. He opened it to reveal an especially large diamond set in a ring. Suddenly the carefully-planned trip to the romantic island made sense: the candlelit dinners; the rose-petal turn-downs. I was usually used to — and happy with — more prosaic accommodation.

"I don't understand," I said.

"Are you going to make me beg?"

"I'd prefer it if you didn't."

"So, then, is that a yes?"

"I'm not sure. It depends what you're asking."

He shrugged, as if he wasn't asking me a question that would change our lives for ever.

"It's yours, the diamond. Whether you want to marry me or not."

I had never been one for jewellery. I didn't like the fuss of accessorising. The same went for marriage. Byron knew all of this, and was asking anyway. I couldn't tell if he was blatantly disregarding my preference or if he had simply decided that his need for me was greater than my disinclination. That was the moment the trouble started.

It wasn't only the unwelcome proposal that had me worried. Worse still, was that I had accepted. Despite the whirring of my cognitive dissonance, the tap-tap-tapping of better judgement against my skull, I agreed to marry Byron. I knew that if I turned him down it would be the end of our relationship, and I wasn't ready for that. Perhaps not immediately, but eventually it would take its toll.

What I didn't guess was that by consenting to his need over mine, it would have the same sad effect. The honeymoon, as they say, was over.

He told me about the money that evening, after a day of stolen glances and tentative affection. I was ribbing him about the size of the diamond, asking if he had had to take a second bond out on his house. Saying the only reason I agreed was the size of the stone: one carat smaller and I would have refused. That's when he told me that he was 'wealthy'. I laughed, saying he could stop trying so hard now, I had already said yes. He was forgetting that I knew him so well, I told him, and that I saw his pilled jerseys and threadbare underwear. Multi-millionaires don't buy toilet paper in bulk, I laughed. But it turned out that they do. I had always known that his company was successful, but had no idea as to the extent. The superfluous funds he kept offshore alone was a hundred times my entire investment portfolio.

The idea of the money came as a warm shock: not unpleasant, but not entirely pleasant either. The revelation, along with the proposal, made my head spin. I understood why he had kept it a secret, but I felt it was duplicitous nonetheless. At a time when you'd expect a couple to feel most intimate, I found our connection vulnerable, stripped away. An exposed wire. Emotionally, I had taken a decisive step backwards, away from Byron. Unfortunately it turned out to be the first of many.

The rest of our time on the island was spent trying to forget about the awkward engagement. Before, we spent leisurely days on the beach, drank *le Dodo* beer in the sun, ate our body weight in ham and cheese galettes and Nutella crêpes, and had lazy afternoon sex. After, we took a helicopter ride over the volcano and the three cirques, went paragliding, and kept busy conscientiously ticking our way through the travel guide's list of must-dos. The diamond was relentless in its glinting.

When we arrived home and settled back into our regular routine, the money was a constant intruder on my thoughts. Not always unwelcome, but ever-present. I knew from reading articles on lottery winners that such a vast amount of un-earned money could be destructive. I refused to be married in community of property, and insisted that we keep our accounts separate. I was a feminist, after all. Byron wanted me to have it all and more — despite giving a significant amount away, he found he always had 'too much.' Like me, he wasn't a great spender. I didn't need it either, I told him, and he laughed. Asked me what the opposite of a gold-digger was, and when I said I didn't know, he said whatever it was, I was that.

Before we had left for Reunion he had his private banker add me as a beneficiary to his current account, and named me as the sole beneficiary in his will. I now had a credit card that I never had to pay off. It was at first disconcerting — I kept thinking that I would have to pay it off *somehow* — then surprisingly liberating.

I no longer stood at a shop shelf and compared products versus prices. If I couldn't decide between the Barista Pinotage (R129) or the Chocolate Block (R168) I would just buy them both. I no longer questioned if we really *needed* a wedge of imported camembert: if I thought we would enjoy it, I bought it. When I saw someone in the queue that looked like they could do with a lucky break, I paid for their (usually) humble basket of groceries. There was a certain freedom in it, and I began to

enjoy the small day-to-day luxuries that it af-
forded. I would also get a kick out of the restraint I
showed. Looking down at my trolley and seeing
the camembert wrapped in its soft foil, and thinking: I have over thirty million rand in the bank today, and I bought a bit of cheese.

The funny thing about the money in the beginning
was that although it made no exceptional difference to my everyday life, it felt like it did. I was
hardly spending more money than I used to, but I
felt rich. I felt a freedom that I had never experienced before, and a security: like a weight I never
knew I had was lifted off my shoulders. It was like
walking around with a warm secret. Being wealthy,
I thought, was more a state of mind than a fat
wallet.

Gradually my reluctance waned. A few years on, I
couldn't remember why I had resisted the fortune
at all.

If anything, I thought I had grown to deserve it by
putting up with Byron's moods. Our relationship,
as I predicted, had deteriorated. We had a good few
years after The Wedding I Never Wanted, but each

year hence seemed less satisfying than the one before it. We tried to buoy it by travelling together,
and that worked for a while. It worked for a cy-
cling trip through Brittany, a walk in Cambodia,
and a swim in Chengdu. On the good days it felt
like we had reconnected for good. It worked less
well for Christmas in New York, a beach holiday in
Thailand, and a cruise to Iceland, and our holiday
in Venice was a disaster. One occasion sums the
trip up: after getting lost over and over again,
Byron submitted to his sore feet, and to his fury,
and sat on a bench, not to speak or be spoken to
for over an hour while I had no choice but to hover
nearby until his darkness had passed.

I had to learn when I could talk to him and when I
couldn't. When he was in a good mood he was his
old funny, charming self. He would spoil me with
flowers and chocolate and put on music and sling
me around the kitchen in a happy dance. We would
plan our next holiday, poring over our travel books
and Google. We'd drink expensive merlot and he'd
kiss me on the lips and surprise me in the shower.
These are the times I could relax and be myself. I
didn't have to consider every word before I said it

out loud. But these moments became more infrequent the longer our relationship progressed. Towards the end, his moods dominated our every interaction. Our house seemed to be carpeted with egg shells. I had to tread accordingly or face his anger, or worse: his contempt.

Our relationship had become complicated. You'd be forgiven for thinking, as an outsider, that the problem was the power in the relationship had shifted to Byron. In fact, the opposite was true. Despite the marriage and the money, all the power was mine for a simple reason: Byron loved me more than I loved him. I realised this when he proposed, and I didn't have the heart to break his. This started as a small struggle, a gentle push-and-pull, but over time it became a tug of war. I knew it, he felt it, and it was to be our sad and slow undoing.

What do you do with a man who loves you too much? I knew leaving would destroy him. If I even hinted at it he would become desperate. He would have anxiety attacks, skip work, drink too much, as if to show me that he couldn't live without me. One particularly dark night, convinced that I was ending the relationship, he threatened suicide. He had a gun, he said, and pills (he had neither). He couldn't live without me. Wouldn't.

I couldn't live this loitering life: my actions dependent on his state of mind. I refused to live in the ripples of his discontent.

I still loved him but the situation had become untenable. It was getting messy, and I don't like mess. I needed an exit plan. One that was as painless as possible for both of us. I loved him too much to leave him, to break his heart.

I knew that I now depended on his money. Before meeting him I was entirely self-sufficient, but since then I had let my career slide, no longer worrying about cash-flow and only taking the jobs that excited me. I couldn't leave the money behind. Gradually, and without me realising it, my perceived financial freedom had become a gilded cage.

It's not like I sat down one day with a notebook and thought of ways to get rid of him. Killing him didn't cross my mind … until it did. Once it was in my head it seemed like the only thing to do. The compassionate thing to do. I would put him out of his suffering; I would do it because I loved him.

Even most beloved pets, I reasoned, were put down when the time came.

One morning he snapped at me for asking what we should have for dinner. He was getting ready for a meeting, removing lint from his jacket.

"I can't think about that now!" he barked.

It was clear, I thought, that his time had come.

Even after I had decided what to do, it took me a long time to action it. It was as if killing him was just a fantasy I would retreat to in times of strife. Something I would imagine at great length but never really do. I'd become one of those old ladies with purple-rinsed hair and rheumy eyes, forever fixated on the life they should have lived. Of course I wouldn't actually *kill him*, I told myself. But I knew, deep down, that it was a lie. Still, I did nothing, as if waiting for one day when I would conveniently find him on the edge of a cliff, where I could give him a quick shove while no one was watching.

I couldn't *plan* something, I thought. It would seem heartless, ruthless. An opportunity would have to present itself. This was perhaps a way of putting it off. Maybe, I thought, I didn't have the courage of my convictions.

I found the box of papers one day while spring-cleaning the house. You'd think, with all the money, that I'd pay someone to do the job, but I liked to do it myself. It gave me immense satisfaction to unpack an entire room, and to clean and de-clutter it. Once a year, I would take a week off work and tick off a room a day. This time, I found the job slightly less satisfying as the rooms were neat and organised to begin with, and, with two days to spare, I decided to attack the space beneath the house.

It's an old house, built over 200 years ago, and while we have made superficial renovations, the core structure has remained the same. At the back of the house there is a small grey wooden door, weathered to the point of crumbling, which is the entry to the small storage space. How a child would love this hobbit-sized door, I thought, as I crept in and began clearing it out. There were to be no children in our future.

It was not all to be thrown away: the dry firewood, laced with spiderwebs, would make excellent fuel for our brazier. Some terracotta pots would do well in our herb garden. There were some lovely old mason jars that we could use in our country-style kitchen. I even kept a sheet of newspaper, finding it quaint, thinking I would have it framed. The most interesting thing I found, however, was a small, ancient-looking clamshell box, dusty black, around the same size as a pack of cigarettes. As I opened it I couldn't help remembering that day on the beach, and the diamond, which still flashed on my finger.

The box held a sheaf of thin off-white papers, that I first took to be cigarette-rolling papers. On closer inspection of the inside of the lid, however, I found a faint stamp: a company logo. A Victorian-era pharmacy. And I knew then how I would kill Byron.

The box seemed to me a gift from fate: the reversal of the original awkward proposal. I enjoyed the aptness of the solution. Sometimes there is poetry in neatness.

I waited till I was alone in the house, then placed one of the delicate papers on a saucer and poured some water over it. After letting it soak for a few hours, I strained the water into an old perfume bottle of mine and discarded the paper. The box of flypapers found refuge in my underwear drawer.

Poisoning your husband is like falling asleep. It happens really slowly and then all at once. Byron never seemed to notice the drops I added to his tea. I came to understand why arsenic was regarded as a tonic in the old days. His eyes became brighter, his cheeks ruddy. Friends commented on his seemingly good health. He complained of some muscle pain, and his stomach gave him trouble.

I started it almost as an experiment, not sure if I would go through with the whole thing. I wasn't at all convinced that I would be able to do it. I gave him the minutest of doses and closely monitored his reaction.

Worried that someone would find the pharmacy box, I threw it away, out of the window on a highway. I kept the flypapers hidden between pages of my novels. A story within a story.

One night it was particularly bad, and I noted to dial it back a little. I couldn't stand to see him in pain. At my insistence he saw a doctor, was diagnosed with gastro-enteritis, and was told to take some time off work and drink plenty of fluids to stay hydrated. He assured the doctor that I made him endless cups of tea.

Over time, the body builds a resistance to arsenic. I had to stop being coy, stop teasing him with it, and get it over with. There was a delicate balance to be observed: I had to do it slowly enough for it to not look suspicious, but at the same time, there had to be, at a some point, a decisive dose. The whole point, after all, was to avoid suffering.

I procrastinated until the day he brought in The Rat. He had a headache, and seemed confused, so I sent him into the garden to read his newspaper while I was preparing a cold chicken salad for lunch. I looked up from carving the bird and screamed. Just outside the kitchen window Byron was standing, staring at me with his shining eyes, holding a dead rat up by its tail. I gripped the handle of the butcher knife, wondering if I would have to use it. He just wanted to show me, he said.

Had I put any rodent poison down? It looks like his stomach exploded, he said. From then on I stopped disposing of the leached flypapers in the compost bin.

A day soon after that, Byron fell ill and had to stay in bed. He could afford the time off. Money kept pouring into our account. I was sitting at his bed-side, reading a book.

"Unsuspecting," he said, his face flushed with fever. I asked him to repeat himself. "Unsuspecting," he said again, and my heart accelerated. Did he know?

"The Unsuspecting Gold-digger," he said. "You know, how we described you. As whatever the opposite of a gold-digger was."

"Or … 'unwitting'?" I tried. "Reluctant?"

"No," he shook his head. "Unsuspecting. It's gold, after all."

The next day, Byron was dead. One moment he had light in his eyes, the next, it was gone. He had a heart attack, brought on, guessed his doctor, by stress. The damage to the heart was clear: there was no need for an autopsy. At the funeral people tut-tutted that success does have its price, and when would we learn to not work so hard? At least there weren't any children, others whispered.

I got home that evening as the storm clouds were gathering. I was glad for the thunder: the house was too quiet without him. Unsettling. I emptied the arsenic water down the drain, double-bagged the perfume bottle and smashed the glass with a meat mallet before throwing it in the neighbour's bin.

I stripped off my plain black dress, heels, and stockings. I left my diamond ring on. I soaked in hot bath while the rain pummelled the roof. The lights flickered a few times, as they do in houses as old as ours. The water soothed my aching feet. I wasn't used to wearing heels. Like I said, I've always been a practical person.

I climbed into bed exhausted, as if I had been awake for years and it was finally time to allow my eyes to close. I swapped my pillow with one that was still scented by Byron, and the lights flickered some more. I checked my bank balance on my phone and then reached for my paperback. It was the same every night: bath, silk pyjamas, bed, bank balance, book. It was a ritual that almost always ensured sound sleep. I opened the novel and the delicate bookmark fluttered out: the last flypaper. I picked it up and dropped it almost immediately, as if it had given me an electric shock. Inscribed on it, in blue ballpoint, was unmistakably Byron's handwriting.

It said "I forgive you."

4

TRAVELLING SLACKS

Trip Advisor Review:

Coconut Bungalows. 4 out of 5 stars.

I had the great pleasure of staying at Coconut Bungalows at the South Coast, KZN, from the 9th to the 13th of October, 2015. It's a wonderful place. Casual, but still refined in the ways that count. One may walk around freely in short sleeves and short pants without fear of lowering the 'standard' of the place. At the same time, the butter for the scones is served at JUST below room temperature (NOT many places get this right) and the tea cups are delivered warm despite the tropical heat of the climate. It's nothing short of miraculous, really, to find these details attended to while it seems that the rest of the country's hospitality industry is slipping as surely as the polar icebergs are melting.

While I am on the topic of scones, I must note that the pastries were incredible. The cakes were tasty and moist; the croissants were a triumph! Lighter scones do not exist except in my memory of my late Aunt Daphne's homely kitchen, where, as a schoolboy, I would gobble them up by the half dozen, much to her delight. "Now hold on, Jeffrey," she would laugh, hugging me to her jiggling bosom, "Leave some for the rest of us, won't you?" I did love my Aunt Daphne.

I found my room unit small but cosy. I would have preferred accommodation that had a sea-view but I was happy enough with the aspect of the flower garden my room offered me. I especially liked the 'outside shower'. I would have preferred air conditioning to a ceiling fan. The king-sized bed was most comfortable. Slightly firmer than I am used to, but I think it was good for my back. My only criticism of the room was that, despite it being kept 'spick and span' by the cleaning staff, a colony of ants seem to have taken up residence in the cupboard. I brought it to the concierge's attention but the problem was not resolved.

The grounds were kept in immaculate condition, and this includes an emerald green lawn that I found myself being quite envious of. Also worth a mention are the just-refurbished tennis courts and the sparkling pool. What a pity the pool was always frothing over with screaming, horse-playing children! I would have quite enjoyed lounging there, taking in some sun, if it weren't for the gremlins continually wetting my newspaper. Luckily, the Coconut Bungalows caters for adults who prefer the company of other adults, and this is why I spent a great deal of my time in the 'Quiet Lounge', where the little beasts couldn't wreak havoc. Of course every now and then a child WOULD enter, seeking a parent, and I would indulge them for a moment. But if it looked as if the child wanted to stay I would clear my throat in an authoritative way, and flick my gaze up to the sign that clearly said 'CHILDREN OUT OF BOUNDS'. If the culpable parent didn't get my subtle hinting, I would slam my book closed and glare at them until they all scampered off. A few guests took exception to my tactics, but the 'Quiet Lounge' is the 'Quiet Lounge', after all, a haven for someone like me, who finds children, even on their best behaviour, vaguely (and, let's be honest, sometimes supremely) irritating. In my opinion those guests should take a long, sober look at themselves and ask the question: why do they think the rules don't apply to them? What kind of children will they raise if they flout instructions like they do? Disrespectful offspring, I can tell you right now, and I observed enough proof of that this holiday.

Irresponsible parents aside, I met some wonderful people at Coconut Bungalows. My regular waiter, Bongani, was a lovely chap. A hundred years old in the shade, but he still managed to bring every single meal to the table piping hot. Slightly deaf, he was, but show me a hundred-year-old man that isn't! I was sure to tip him generously at the end of my stay.

The food was certainly above expectations and there wasn't a menu I wasn't happy with, apart from the Thursday lunch, which was a make-your-own-pasta dish. In all honesty I considered it quite cheeky, to expect the guests to cook their own food after paying full board. I have never been a fan of spaghetti.

The coffee was good, but not great. I will take my own blend next time. I did however appreciate the option of warm and cold milk at the beverage station.

The only other complaint I have regarding mealtimes is that there was one particular guest at the table adjacent to mine who INSISTED on (breast!)feeding her baby right at the table! As if common decency had never occurred to her. I found it downright rude and indecent and I told Bongani so, but I don't think he heard. It honestly makes me wonder, sometimes, about the future of the human race. Are we doomed to a vulgar existence where just about anything goes? It was quite upsetting to me, as you can probably tell.

On the subject of inconsiderate neighbours, the dark chap staying in the bungalow next to mine would perform a sort of dance every morning at sunrise, on a rolled out carpet. I wouldn't have minded except that this exercise of his seemed to chase away the birds I was trying to view with my new binoculars. When I asked him to stop he just mumbled something in some oriental language which I'm quite sure he knew I wouldn't understand. Oh, well, perhaps I am in an overly generous mood but I can't fault the owners of Coconut Bungalows for this particular source of vexation. It's not like they can keep 'those' kinds of people out.

The much vaunted 'nature walks' were a slight disappointment. Although the trails are indeed very scenic, the routes are not well signposted and a walk that should have taken 45 minutes took me 3 hours and I was most put out to be told that I had missed my afternoon tea. This, I found unacceptable, and it spoiled the rest of my day.

To end on a positive note, I would like to mention that the private beach attached to the bungalows was most beautiful and pristine. I enjoyed my daily walks along the shore.

What is left to say except that despite some hiccups and minor setbacks, I had a most marvellous stay at Coconut Bungalows, and I give them a well-deserved rating of 4 stars out of 5. I will certainly be returning in the future.

Jeffrey Sacks, AKA @travellingslacks

Dear Travelling Slacks

Thank you for taking the time to write such a long and incredibly detailed review. We are glad that you had a (mostly) wonderful stay and look forward to welcoming you back. I would, however, like to address your various points of discontent.

With regards to your bungalow: On booking your room for your stay you were offered an upgrade to a larger unit with air conditioning and a sea view for a marginal fee, which you declined. Thus, I don't understand why, in your review, you say you would have preferred a larger room. Perhaps next time you will accept the offer of an upgrade.

I have passed on your compliments to our pastry chef. She will be delighted that her scones reminded you of a warm childhood memory. I dare say it won't come as a surprise, however, as she did mention that her baked goods disappeared at quite a rate in the week that you stayed with us.

I apologise again for the ant problem, however, the cleaning staff did report to me that the stash of scones and biscuits you kept in your cupboard was the reason the colony kept returning, despite our house rule that there is no food to be kept in the rooms (for this very reason). The leaking bottle of Baileys that you brought from home exacerbated the problem. Coconut Bungalows offers full board, 3 meals a day, plus morning and afternoon tea, and a full bar. There is also a room service, so you should never have worried about going hungry or thirsty. In fact, most of our guests complain that we feed them too much! Perhaps if you obey our rule, we will be able to avoid the insect problem on your next stay with us.

I'm sorry that you felt the boisterous children spoilt the pool for you. Coconut Bungalows is marketed as a fun, energetic, whole-family resort. I assume you would have gathered that from our website when you made your reservation, as it is full of pictures of 'screaming, horse-playing' children. I am glad that you found relative peace in our Quiet Lounge.

I have passed on your glowing praise of your

waiter to him. Bongani thanks you for the R10 tip you left him for the 5 days of 3-meals-a-day service. He tells me that he did offer to make the pasta sauce for you on Thursday's make-your-own-pasta meal, but that you refused. We find that one interactive meal a week is a fun thing to do, and gets our guests chatting amongst themselves and making friends. I'm sorry it did not hold much appeal for you. In future we will warn you of the occasion and you won't have to participate; our chefs will make something special for you in advance.

Bongani also related the story of your disapproval of your fellow guest breastfeeding her baby at the table behind yours. At first I didn't understand the problem. If the woman was behind you, why was she in your line of sight? Even if you did manage to glimpse her, Bongani assured me — despite it being necessary, in my opinion — that the lady covered up and fed her baby most discreetly. He also told me that he offered you another table on the other side of the restaurant, but that you did not want to move. I'm not certain, then, what the actual problem was, but I trust Bongani made certain that you were comfortable. He did tell me that he stopped 'hearing' this particular complaint on the 3rd or 4th occasion. On a side note I must tell you that Bongani is famous for his selective hearing.

I'm sorry you weren't a fan of our coffee. I will let The Roast Beanery — the most highly regarded coffee supplier in the country — know that their particular brand is not your favourite.

Our nature walks are clearly signposted, there are maps at reception, and a hiking guide is always available at a small fee. Perhaps next time you can take advantage of a guide's assistance and make your way back in time for afternoon tea.

Lastly, regarding your neighbour: Professor Abdullah is a loyal and much-respected guest at Coconut Bungalows. He doesn't speak any 'oriental' languages, so I assume what you heard was English. His sunrise 'dance' was, in fact, his morning prayers. The Prof was extremely gracious in that he never once complained about your eccentric habits, such as playing your violin whenever the fancy took you, your loud, drunken conversations with yourself in the middle of the night, the ants you brought into the area, the immodest Speedo you wore for your daily beach walks, and/or the way you showered in the front of the unit, naked, in full view of the rest of the bungalows. For future reference, the spout you used as an 'outside shower' is really just a tap to assist you in rinsing off beach sand before entering your unit.

Thanking you again for your detailed and exhaustive review.

Kind Regards, Suzy Dos Santos, Owner, Coconut Bungalows

Trip Advisor Review:

REVISED: Coconut Bungalows. 3 out of 5 stars.

Dear 'Suzy'

Thank you for your reply to my honest review of your establishment. I suppose not every owner enjoys it when their guests engage in 'straight talking'! As you can see I have downgraded my rating of Coconut Bungalows from 4 to 3 stars (out of 5), as your response reminded me of other niggles that I thought best forgotten in the original generosity I was feeling when first writing the review. I also feel that the passive aggression in your reply warranted a drop in ratings, as you clearly do not understand nor follow the very important maxim that 'the customer is always right'!

I won't stoop to your level by addressing every separate point of contention, however I must address one or two issues that I take exception to.

The first is the issue of that rude woman who insisted on breastfeeding her baby right under my nose. Yes, her table was behind mine, but just because I couldn't SEE her actually feeding the child doesn't mean I wasn't aware of it happening behind my back. Yes, she may have covered up her actual breasts while feeding the child, but what use is that, when everyone around her can imagine what is happening under the cover! There are many places that are suitable for a mother to feed an infant: her bungalow, being one! And let me tell you, her feeding was not confined to the dining area either. I saw her doing it on the outside terrace during sundowners and at the pool, too! Bongani was not the only staff member with selective hearing: everyone I complained to just shrugged it off, which I found disrespectful and patronising.

And, yes, I did see the pictures of the raucous children on the website when I booked my accommodation, but I assumed, albeit mistakenly so, that the Coconut Bungalows would strive to accommodate ME and MY particular needs, too.

On another note. Your sarcasm with regards to my taste in coffee did not go unnoticed. The Roast Beanery's coffee is indeed the best in the country. Perhaps you are just not preparing it correctly?

With regards, Jeffrey Sacks, AKA @travellingslacks

Dear Mr Sacks

Perhaps you can send us your notes on how to prepare coffee? We've always been under the impression that you add hot water, brew, and strain, or use the espresso machine. Are we missing something? Is there, in fact, a superior way to make coffee? Please let us know.

It has come to my attention via my cleaning staff that various items from your room are missing. I wonder, did you accidentally pack some of our Coconut Bungalow towels into your luggage? We are also short one cotton bathrobe, a small pillow, a bottle opener, and the large pump-action bottles of shampoo and body wash that we provide for guests to make use of, but not to take home. If you do have these items, please let me know and I will arrange a courier to collect them from you. Alternatively, I can send you the bill to replace the missing things.

Regarding the issue of the guest who was breast-feeding in public: We were so pleased to see that she felt comfortable enough at the Coconut Bunga-lows to feed her baby wherever and whenever the baby was hungry. Being a new mother is an ex-hausting job, and we were glad to see her and her little one happy and relaxed. This was more of a compliment to us than any online review.

On the subject, I have taken the liberty of looking up your reviews on various other establishments and am happy I did so. I see your other complaints are in a similar vein. If my memory serves me correctly, one guest relations officer, in particular, offered to gag you and smash your violin over your head to curtail further complaints from his other guests. I thought it was a rather violent thing to say, but I am beginning to come around to his way of thinking.

I wonder, Mr Sacks, what the real problem is. Are you lonely? Do writing these reviews make you feel more important? At first I thought you were a man of fine taste, noticing the softness of the butter, the lightness of the scones. But now I see that you're just … well, it appears that you have nothing better to do than to bully the mostly lovely owners of South African travel destinations.

I take back what I said about being happy to welcome you back to Coconut Bungalows. You can keep your R10 tips and your violin and your indecent exposure and your pilfered ant-trailing cookies. You were a disaster of a guest and the truth is that we really don't want you to come back. Ever.

PS. Here's a tip for you: The next time you see a woman breastfeeding a baby and it offends you,

STOP LOOKING. Also: STOP WEARING A SPEEDO.

Suzy Dos Santos, Owner, Coconut Bungalows

Trip Advisor Review:

REVISED: Coconut Bungalows. 2 out of 5 stars.

Dear 'Suzy'

I suppose I should have expected this childish response. Not everyone can take constructive criticism. I find that women, in particular, battle with this. I wonder if I should be having this conversation with your husband, instead. I have told everyone I know about your ghastly communication, and I won't be surprised if, going forward, you see a steep decline in your reservations.

With regards, Jeffrey Sacks, AKA @travellingslacks

Dear Mr Sacks

What my husband knows about the hospitality industry is scary, seeing as he is an investment banker, so I doubt you'd have much luck there. I wonder if I should be having a word with your wife? Perhaps offering my commiseration, at being married to you? I saw a picture of her and thought she looked vaguely Russian. I wondered if you really have a wife — why was she not travelling with you? — or if it was just a photo that you found somewhere on Google images. I looked at your Facebook page and you are welcome to let your small group of friends know not to visit us.

In addition, I have sent your guest profile to all the establishments I know, warning them to not accept a reservation from you. I forwarded the same message to the South African Board of Tourism. If, in future, you can't get a reservation ANYWHERE, you will know why.

I have attached the bill for the items you stole from the room. Please send me the proof of payment at your earliest convenience.

Suzy Dos Santos, Owner, Coconut Bungalows

Trip Advisor Review:

REVISED: Coconut Bungalows. 1 out of 5 stars.

Dear 'Suzy'

As you can see I have downgraded your rating to 1 out of 5 stars. I find your attitude entirely unsatisfactory.

Jeffrey Sacks, AKA @travellingslacks

Dear Jeffrey

You can take your one star and shove it.

Suzy

Trip Advisor Review:

REVISED: Coconut Bungalows. 0 out of 5 stars.

Dear 'Suzy'

The star has been 'shoved'!

Jeff

~

Dear Jeff

Please stop emailing me. I think this has gone far enough.

Suzy

~

Dear Suzy

You have no idea how far I can take this.

Jeff

~

Jeff

Seriously. Step away from your computer. I will no longer be answering your emails.

Suzy

Suzy

I will not be ignored!

Jeff

Suzy? Suzy? I demand an answer!

Dear Suzy

I am going to email you every single day of your life unless you answer me.

Jeff

Jeff

I have called the police and laid an harassment charge against you, as well as one for theft and indecent exposure. They said they will pay you a visit. We have your address on file. It would be in your best interest to stop contacting me.

PS. We have photos of you streaking in your 'outside shower' and we will use them against you if we have to. I hope it doesn't come to that.

Suzy

~

Dear Suzy

You're right. It's because I'm lonely. Please drop the charges.

Jeff

~

Jeff

Loneliness is no excuse for being an utter asshole. Didn't your Aunt teach you that?

Suzy

Suzy

You're right, she did. She was a wonderful woman. I used to gobble up all her scones and she'd say: "Hold on, now, Jeffrey, leave some for the rest of us!" How I loved my Aunt Doris.

Jeff

Jeff

Wasn't your aunt's name 'Daphne'?

Suzy

Suzy

You're right. It's Daphne.

Jeff

Jeff, you don't have an aunt Daphne, do you? You made her up.

Jeff? You there?

The host server @travellingslacks is not recognised. This email address has been deleted. This message will not be re-sent. This is a permanent error message.

5

SOMETHING BORROWED

I cover my nose and mouth with the ivory silk of the gown and inhale deeply. I want to remember every detail of this day. I run my hand over the beaded bodice: a love letter in Braille. I sit down at the dressing room table and start pinning up my hair. I had it set in generous curls yesterday. The diamanté clips sparkle as I move my head. My make-up is laid out in front of me.

I begin with foundation. Painting my face, I feel like I am performing a rite of passage. This careful, slow transformation, from wide-eyed child-girl to woman. The butterflies start beating their wings:

they are in my stomach and in my head. Thoughts alight and flutter away again before I, breathless, can catch them.

It will soon be time to leave for the church. Pop will be coming in the family Bentley to pick us up. He took it out earlier to have it washed and polished. He wanted it to shine like me, he said. He's done so much for Ruth and I; it will be nearly impossible to say goodbye.

At least Pop likes Raymond. That will make leaving home easier. Raymond is like the son Pop never had. They watch cricket and drink beer together. After lunch on Sunday afternoons they sit in the golden light on the verandah, hands behind their heads, in a haze of comfortable silence.

Raymond asked Pop's permission for my hand a week before he proposed to me. How he kept that secret for a whole week I'll never know. Seven breakfasts, seven lunches, seven dinners and Pop didn't do so much as wink at me.

It was a Summer night when Raymond took me to the beach. The sand was still warm. I wore a new skirt. It trembled in the evening breeze. Raymond spoke about the day we met and how much he had grown to love me, and my family. We started to kiss and the world turned on its side. I wondered, then, if that would be the moment I'd give myself to him: that perfect night under the stars. But Raymond had other plans. His hand unfurled like a flower to reveal the diamond he had brought: it had been his grandmother's. It sparkles on my finger now. I was mute but Raymond knew the answer was yes. He is my first and only love. I could marry no one but him.

When I told Ruth she said she was happy for me but I saw the hurt in her eyes. Being older, she imagined she would be the first one to get married. She chafed under Pop's strict house rules. She was always the independent one. On sticky nights she used to tell me her dreams of moving out of the family house, out of the town where everyone's nose was in everyone else's business. Moving to a completely new place, perhaps in Europe somewhere: Italy, Spain, France. Some place she could be herself. She's my maid of honour today. She has the prettiest green dress.

Ruth introduced me to Raymond. Not in that way:

not on purpose. She had taken me along to a picnic with some college friends of hers and there he was, fawning all over her. He watched Ruth with such a determined look in his eyes. I asked her, afterwards, if they were together. She had just laughed and shook her head, her bob swaying.

I bumped into Raymond a few weeks later, at the MonteVista cinema. He remembered me – bought me popcorn and a bag of winegums – as if I was his kid sister. He introduced me to his tall friends and said something to make everyone laugh. My cheeks burned with the memory of how often I had thought of him since the picnic. He pretended not to notice.

I can't remember which film was on that night – my own had been playing in my head. Nothing original: Handsome boy meets plain girl at picnic to the soundtrack of the Beatle's 'Day Tripper'. The universe conspires to bring them together once again at a local haunt. Handsome boy burrows his way into girl's uncompromising father's heart, drops on knee, and story ends in confetti and general wedded bliss.

In the end, our story wasn't quite as twee as that, but it wasn't far off. Raymond was always the perfect gentleman and Pop couldn't help but love him. He was part of the family before he ever asked for my hand.

I was so besotted with Raymond that I offered myself to him. It was the only way I could reconcile the overwhelming feelings I had. When Pop stopped insisting on a chaperone we would have moments alone: in the corner of a garden at a party; against the rough black bark of a tree during an evening walk. Once in the bedroom of a relative, breathless. I was ready each time but Raymond used to stop himself before my cardigan was unbuttoned.

I want him so much sometimes I want to crawl under his skin. I wish I could get inside his body the way he is inside my mind.

Tonight will be the night. The butterflies have strayed south.

I miss my mom. Of course, this is the time a girl misses her mom. Would she have told me what to expect on my wedding night? Or would she just primly pat me on the shoulder? Either would be fine with me. All I crave is her presence. Pop has tried his best but there are only so many ribbons a father can tie in his daughter's hair. The funeral was the last family function. The wedding planning has brought some sunshine into the house.

I begin curling my eyelashes. Ruth taught me how to do it. Ruth taught me how to do most things. How to blot my lipstick so that it doesn't come off on everything, how to ice my eyebrows before I pluck, how to stop a run in my stockings with a dab of nail polish. And then other things; things that will come in handy tonight. She has always been so generous with her femininity. I apply mascara and separate my lashes. I wonder what's taking Pop so long? I push my face right up to the mirror to examine it. My reflection mists over as I breathe.

With a nervous inhalation I decide it's time to put on my dress. Before I take it down from the hanger I admire it one last time. I stand there in my corset and stockings thinking that it's the most exquisite dress I've ever seen. I step into it carefully and pull it up. I have to wriggle a little to get it over my hips. It's a little tighter than the last time I tried it on. No matter. The zip slides up without hesitation.

I put my shoes on. I battle with the tiny buckle, it's too delicate for my fingers. By the time I look into the mirror the vision is complete. It's everything I've dreamed about.

There's a gentle knock on the door. Only Ruth knocks like that.

"Come in!" I sing, my heart near bursting.

The door opens. It is Ruth, but she's not wearing her pretty green dress. She looks old and tired.

"Is everything okay?" I ask. "You're not dressed for the wedding."

Her face is a mask of despair.

"I'm not kidding, Ruthie," I say playfully. "Pop will be here any minute."

She cannot talk.

"Ruth? What's wrong?"

Her shoulders stoop. She walks to the bed and sits down. Her head disappears in her hands.

"What is it?" I say, starting to worry, wondering what could make her act this way. She looks up at me with so much pain in her eyes that I have to look away. I go to the window and watch the sky. I need some air. I try to open the window but there is a padlock on it.

"Where did you find it?" asks Ruth.

"Find what?"

"That wedding dress. That. Damn. Wedding dress."

Her voice is gruff and I don't know what she means.

"I don't understand," I say.

"Not again, Emily, please, not again."

She's driving me mad! "What on earth are you talking about?"

"What am I talking about?" she says, "What have we been talking about for the past fifty years?"

I'm frustrated now. I feel the beginning of tears but

I blink them back. I don't want to ruin my make-up.

"I hid that dress away!" she fumes. "I don't know how you found it. Take it off!"

She claws at me, at the beaded bodice. I push her away.

"I'll get rid of it properly, this time. I will shred it, and burn it, and bury it, and make sure it will never haunt us again!"

"No!" I shriek. "Why would you do that? Why would you say such an awful thing?"

"Because I love you. Because I can't take these episodes of yours any longer."

My mind is racing. Ruth's eyes arrest mine.

"Try to remember, Em."

I start to feel the sharp metal edges of hysteria.

"Remember what?"

"Remember what happened, fifty years ago."

"How can I? I wasn't born yet!"

Ruth shakes her head.

"You were twenty-two years old! It was your wedding day."

"But today is my wedding day."

I look out of the window again. My eyes fall to the locked pane. Ruth's cold fingers turn my head.

"Look at me, Emily! Look at my face. I'm an old lady!"

She does look old. Her hair is grey! I recoil in shock. "What happened to your hair?"

She is gentle now. "Come, look in the mirror."

"No!" I shout. I don't want that white hair, those pale wrinkles.

Ruth grabs a hand mirror off the dressing room table. She forces the image on me. "Look!"

The face I see is ravaged. A cracked doll's face. A cruel caricature.

My heart is beating fast, too fast.

"Where is Raymond?" I ask.

Ruth's anger drains out of her. "He died, Em."

I don't believe her. How can I?

"He was killed in a car accident, on the way to the wedding."

I am sick with shock. I run into to bathroom and heave into the toilet.

Mental images, blurry at first, assault me: Raymond's mother's anguished face at his funeral; the sickly sweet smell of the lily wreath; being assailed by condolence cards, some arriving months after his death. Nightmares of his crushed body. Broken, bloody.

I heave again. Then more harrowing pictures: Another funeral, this time we're the ones throwing soil on the coffin.

"Pop?" I ask.

Ruth is crying now.

. . .

"He was in the other car."

Yes. I remember now.

Everyone had said how awful the coincidence had been. What bad luck. Unbelievable, they said. Impossible. But not.

The dress is heavy on me now. My skin itches. I feel like I can't breathe. I struggle with it. Ruth comes over to help. I see the strain on her face. Once I am free of it she holds me and soothes me.

"It's over now," she coos, stroking my hair. "Everything will be okay."

It's an old, battered promise.

With a rush of heat I remember something else. The reason Pop was speeding away in his car. The reason he lost control and drove into the bridge, followed in desperate pursuit by Raymond. Passion allows no time for safety belts or following distance.

Pop had gone over to Raymond's house with a gift. A fatherly premarital gesture, but the intimate words caught in his throat when he saw Raymond's tousled hair, and Ruth's green dress slung carelessly over the settee. Ten minutes later they exploded in a mess of tar and broken glass.

I look up at Ruth. The lines of regret etched into her skin. She looks at me expectantly, waiting, dreading the next, inevitable, part of the story. But I see she has suffered enough, and she is my sister.

I won't remember that part today.

6

SHE DID IT

The suspect.

The suspect has one eye swollen shut and blood highlights in her yellow hair. A split lip that sticks so far out that I want to tuck it back into her face for her. What makes dried blood black? What makes eye-skin swell so hard that it buries its own eyeball? Cannibalistic gesture or measure of protection? Too late, eye socket, too late. The suspect stares into space. Saliva shines her chin. She isn't aware of the drool. She's numb. If she's lucky, she's numb. She stares and stares and doesn't see anything.

There is nothing to see here.

She has seen enough.

The suspect was admitted last night. It wasn't the first time.

The suspect? you are thinking. Surely you mean *the victim?*

No, I mean The Suspect. She was found in a puddle of blood. It was mostly her husband's.

What kind of love is this? When the couple's red stuff runs together in tributaries and streams, mixing and morphing into a dark lake of glue. What kind of love is this? Or, more correctly, what kind of love *was* this? For it is no more.

When did it end? When did the crimson petal turn to brown? When did the suspect's skull go from whole to cracked? Now there is a spiderweb, a snowflake etched into the bone. You know the story. But maybe not the whole story. Maybe not the exact story. Every snowflake is unique.

His skull was cracked, too. The husband's. More

smashed than 'cracked'. A whole piece of head bone was missing, like a seashell eroded by the sand and tide. I expected to find a sea-brined brain, but it was messier than that. No cool rinsing saline, but instead: hot air and insects. Not too many: there wasn't enough time between the deed and the damning. Just a couple of fat black flies. Their wings vibrating right into our itchy ears.

Blunt force trauma. That old chestnut. We looked around for the instrument (and the puzzle-piece of skull) but it didn't reveal itself. It did not jump up and dance. Isn't it funny that we call it an 'instrument'? As if we could pick it up on a whim and play a tune. A death ditty. A melody of murder. I wonder which song was on when this gory thing was playing out. This blunt game. Every crime has a soundtrack.

She had looked dead, too, until all of a sudden she wasn't. Mottled. Smashed up, but alive. She gasped and chucked up blood, like a possessed puppet in a horror show. Like a victim of an exorcism. But not a victim. Not only a victim, anyway. A suspect, too.

Yes, you can be both. Her husband was both, too. Who else would engrave the snowflake on his wife's skull? Who else would swell her lip? A third party! I hear you shout. An intruder! An evil bastard intent on grievous bodily harm.

It's possible. I have learnt that anything is possible. But evil almost always pitches up at the door with a housecoat on. A comfy old housecoat that smells of home and is invariably scabbed by custard and a snailtrail of last week's roast chicken gravy.

Child molested? You want to blame the ice-cream truck man. (It wasn't him.)

Girl raped? You point a finger at the faceless trenchcoat. (It wasn't him.)

Woman battered to within an inch of her life (and sometimes outside of it) — you see the perpetrator as one of The Others. It wasn't them. Mostly, it wasn't them. Mostly, it was the father, the uncle, the husband. Mostly the evil is deeply seeded inside our circles of love. That's what makes it truly evil.

The suspect lifts a broken finger to the shorn part of her scalp. Runs a dirty fingernail above her ear. What is she thinking about? Is she replaying last night's events? Is the glimmer of light on her stitched-up face the reflection of the story? How much does she know, and of that, how much will she tell us?

'Mrs Long?' I say, for the third time. Triad, trilogy, troika. Third time lucky, although not for her. She hears me — I can see the faint flicker — but still she keeps staring at the wafer coloured walls. Hospital equipment rattles down the corridor. Metal trollies, and needles scratching paper. Someone's blood pressure cuff exhales.

'Janine?' I say. It tastes wrong, but it does the trick. She cranes her stiff neck in my direction. One eyeball swivels. It's a pretty eyeball. The other is still a prisoner. She opens her lip-balloons to speak but nothing comes out.

DOESN'T ANSWER TO MARRIED NAME, I write in my notebook. It's not the standard police-issue notebook. Those are useless. I like my books tightly bound. When it comes to notebooks, I appreciate strict bondage. When it comes to sex: not so much. I have tied up enough criminals to put me off handcuffs in the bedroom for good.

A ghost of a word escapes her mouth. Then another, then another. Three spook words. A phantom triangle. A triple spectre switchback. Things happen in threes. This is true. I strain my ears. I prime my hammer, anvil and stirrup. I am ready to listen. Not just to hear, but to listen. There is a distinct difference.

I see her teeth are broken, too. That wasn't in the report. Perhaps they were not able to open her mouth when she first came in. Perhaps it had been clamped. Perhaps the horror had wired it shut.

TEETH, I write down.

BROKEN.

I clear my throat.

'Could you … would you repeat that?' I say in the most gentle voice I possess. It does not come easy. It sounds like a grizzly bear trying to sing a lullaby.

It does not come naturally to me. Look at me. Look at me! I am not a tender man.

Of course, it *could* have been an intruder. This is Johannesburg, after all. Sunny South Africa. We are nothing if not a long-festering abscess boiling over with the hot pink pus and frantic squirming oily maggots of crime and violence. And don't you dare act disgusted. It is your doing as much as it is mine. If you take exception to anything it should be your own indifference. At least I am here, in this hospital room. At least I am getting my rough hands dirty.

It could have been a faceless stranger who burst into this couple's bedroom and gave them matching head traumas. He could've handed them identical blows, one for him, one for her. Two for the price of one. Like monogrammed velour bathrobes made in China, His and Hers. Or those old married people who have been together too long and wear matching twinsets with pictures of snowy mountains embroidered on the fronts, replete with a smelly nanny goat, a copper bell at her throat. It could have been *Die Swart Gevaar,* but my gut tells me otherwise. I'd stake my balls on it. And

I don't do that lightly. I'd very much like to keep my balls just where they are.

I hand the suspect a plastic beaker with a bendy straw. She won't be eating for a while. She is getting all the hydration and nutrients she needs from her IV but that won't stop her mouth from being as a dry as these wafer walls. She blinks her solitary eye at me in thanks, and slurps. Her injuries do not make for delicate drinking. There is more chin-dribble. In another lifetime, in another story, in a parallel universe I would take a soft cotton cloth and wipe her face for her. I would hold her. Tell her that the worst is over. That she's going to be okay.

But we're not on that particular planet. We're here in this beige private ward and she is the suspect and I am the cop and I need to find out what the hell happened to the purple corpse in the refrigerator drawer that is wearing a wedding ring with her name on it.

I take the beaker back. It's time to talk. I need to hear those three words again to make sure that I didn't imagine them. I angle my body towards her. I steeple my fingers. I wait. I don't tap my feet.

She takes a breath, and then winces at the ribs that curl around her chest like an ivory cage for her heart. Those bones are engraved, too. When I read the medical report I pictured her as a scribbled-on skeleton. Old and new fracture scars running all over her bone and crunchy cartilage like a roadmap to oblivion. How many ribs has she broken? How many arms, legs, cheekbones? How many times can you break a limb before it just won't heal anymore? How many times can you shatter a pelvis before it just gives in and gives up? I pictured her as a tattooed skeleton; so when I came in here I was surprised by her skin and hair. Her modest padding. Her beautiful eyeball.

'I did it,' she says again.

I go back to the top of the page where, hours before I had met her, I had written SHE DID IT.

It wasn't rocket science. I didn't even think it through. Sometimes the deep gut / balls combination just does the work for you. If you can't trust the deep gut / balls combination then you can't trust anything. The penis, on the other hand, the shaft, is another story altogether.

SHE DID IT, I had scrawled in shouty uppercase, sure and arrogant, as if it were a title for a new screenplay, or a song. I tick the words. The ink mark is an inverted shark fin.

Her breathing is shallow from the nerves or the hesitation to re-rupture the ribs. She shouldn't be in this much pain. They should give her some more painkillers. I wanted her *compos mentis* for the questioning, but I'm not a sadist. Besides, I have what I need. I only needed those three words. The rest is backstory. The rest doesn't matter. I ring the bell for the nurse.

The suspect turns towards me, with some effort, and I am confronted by her whole face at once. Or, at least, a face that used to be whole. A face that will never be whole again. It's quite a picture. I will myself to not blink, to not turn away from the mess. To not squirm before the crazy quilt that is her new skin. I need to take responsibility for her condition. It was one of us, after all, that did this to her. A fellow human. A fellow man. Kin, but not kindred.

'I killed him,' she says. 'I killed him.'

She turns her attention back to the beige. I wait for the tears. I wait for her to start rocking and heaving. I wait for her to paint herself with tar. She just stares at the wall. Just when I think that he has finally knocked her into catatonia, she wipes perspiration from her hands and lows in discomfort.

A decade rolls by like ancient grey tumbleweed and a nurse finally arrives.

'Took long enough,' I mumble. He ignores me. What is it about medical people being indifferent to pain? Is it because they see too much of it? Do they become numb by choice or necessity? Can't they see that this woman has been through enough? Look at her! Her skeleton is a scribble! I want to yell at him. Where is the fucking morphine?

His nurse's uniform remains stubbornly starched in slow motion.

You think she's making it up? I want to yell. *You think she's faking it?*

Why am I not indifferent to the pain? I must see more suffering than these people. That is why I smell of the streets and not the dry mist of alcoholic hand sanitiser. I am agitated by their too-clean tunics and their flat empathy. As if they remove their understanding along with the bacteria on their hands. As if they set themselves apart from us, the sad, sorry, roiling society. Quickly! Sanitise! Before you catch it. Before you catch a germ of empathy.

'She's had as much as she's allowed,' he says, looking at the chart at the foot of her bed. 'The next dose will be in two hours.'

The suspect's fists drip with sweat.

Fuck that. Fuck what's *allowed*.

I take a step towards the nurse. I am not a small man.

'Give her more,' I say. 'Now.'

I will be damned if I will allow another man to cause this woman any more unnecessary pain.

I think he's going to stand up to me. I am ready for it, but then he collects a small bag of clear liquid and hooks it up to her IV line. He leaves. I sit and watch it trickle. I urge the plastic bladder to empty faster. It is too slow. Too slow.

But then the groaning stops. Gradually the fists unfurl; blossoming finger flowers. Colour leaks back into her cheeks. We both breathe again.

I offer her more water; she refuses.

'Is there anything else you'd like to say?' I ask.

I need to get away. I didn't mean to spend so long here in this antiseptic purgatory. I have a job to do. I have other blood to sniff.

She swallows. She says, again: 'I killed him.'

'I know,' I say. 'I know.'

I don't want her to feel guilty. What I really want to say is: *I'm glad you killed the sonofabitch.*

I want to say: *I wish you'd done it sooner. Before he broke you in half.*

There is something pulling at her face, at her balloons. I don't want her to cry. I don't want to watch her stretch her stitched-up face. But there is no water in her eyes. The twitching of the lips is not weeping. It is relief. It is triumph. Her eye has stars in it. She has survived.

I start my banged-up Hilux with a twist of key, as if I am turning a dagger in someone's stomach. I can't help the violence of my thoughts. Occupational hazard. My soul has seen too much to be pure. I drive out of the hospital after paying R8 for parking. Bastards, I think, for making the worried and the grieving pay to visit their loved ones. Does no-one in this money-grubbing city have a fucking conscience?

The chevron boom shudders skyward. I accelerate, leaving the beautiful eyeball behind. The sensation of the tyres' traction on the road is good. I feel like I could drive forever on an open road. Instead I'm hemmed in by traffic-tense zippers and clouds of carbon dioxide, and I almost get T-boned by a taxi with gravel for brakes. Red lights are regarded as a suggestion rather than a rule. No point telling Metro. I wave the taxi off with my middle finger. If he takes exception he can take it up with the Glock I have resting in sweat-softened leather against my ankle. I have enough warm bullets for everyone.

'She did it,' says Domino. I can't remember why I call him that. It's not like he is freckled, or especially entertaining. He's not even Italian. He nudges the file into my hand. He wants me to look at it again.

'Of course she did it,' I say. 'I thought you had something new to tell me.'

'Oh, I do,' he says. He is grandstanding, smug, but I don't know why. Had I missed an important detail at the crime scene?

'Did you know that he broke her teeth, too?' I say.

'Did he?' says Domino. It's not a question.

I can feel the minutes ticking by. I have wasted enough time today. I need to get some action. I need to slam a body against my car's bonnet. I wouldn't mind firing my gun, either.

'It's not what it seems,' Dom says. 'You need to look closer.'

'Look closer? She killed her husband in self defence. The details don't matter.'

'The details always matter,' says Dom, as if he is a wise master edifying a recalcitrant student. As if he is goddamned Mr Miyagi. 'You just don't want to see it.'

'Spit it out,' I say, looking at my watch. 'I'm getting old.'

'Maybe if you stopped falling in love with your suspects you'd have a clearer head.'

I take the folder to the restaurant down the road. Their coffee is good but their food is terrible. They know to not bother me with a menu. I start from page one of the file contents and make sure I take in every word. Halfway through my second cup I see the note about broken teeth. So it was in there. I did miss it. What else did I miss? I keep going. My stomach buzzes. I ignore it. I have another cup and I start to get the caffeine-sweats. I hate the caffeine-sweats. My mind begins to wander and then I see it. A psychiatrist's name. A telephone number.

'You saw Janine Long?' I say into the handset. 'She was a patient of yours?'

The doctor won't discuss her on the phone. I grab my keys and leave a pink note on the table.

'A troubled young woman,' he says to me. I am still sweating.

'A walking cliché,' I say. Not that she's walking anywhere at the moment.

We're in his consulting room that smells of vanilla beans and dollar signs.

'You think all young women are troubled?' he asks.

'I think everyone is troubled,' I say. 'It's the human condition.'

The psychiatrist doesn't disagree. I guess we've both witnessed the ugly.

'Let me guess,' I say. 'I'm going to need a court order before you discuss her particular troubles with me?'

'Not necessarily,' he says, uncrossing his legs. 'What do you need to know?'

'I need to know why she came to in a pool of blood this morning.'

'Her own blood?' asks the doc.

'Some of it was.'

'The rest was … the husband's?'

'Yes.'

'Ah,' the doctor says. 'She killed him? Let me guess: self defence?'

'Yes,' I say. 'Self defence.'

'Ah.'

'You're not surprised?'

'I'm afraid not.'

'You knew it would happen,' I say, 'and you didn't think to notify the authorities?'

'Of course I notified the authorities,' he says. 'How do you think you got my number?'

'How long did the abuse go on for?' I ask.

'I believe it started when she was 14.'

'14? She knew the victim — her husband-to-be — when she was 14?'

The shrink shakes his head. Begins to say something, then stops.

'Then,' I say, 'there were others?'

It wouldn't be the first time a woman chose one abuser after another. Like being slung out of one revolving door to be sucked straight into the next. The doctor looks confused. He leans forward, resting his elbows on his thighs.

'Who exactly,' he says carefully, 'do you think the abuser is?'

'Was,' I say. 'It *was* her husband.'

His face pops with surprise.

'No,' he says. 'No, not at all!'

It's my turn to look confused. I don't like it.

'Mrs Long suffered from Munchausen Syndrome. That's when — '

'I know what Munchausen is,' I say. 'But it doesn't add up.'

'You're thinking of Munchausen in its narrowest form. It comes in many strains.'

'I don't understand.'

'Mrs Long wouldn't be happy until she was hospitalised. She learnt to do significant damage so that she wouldn't be turned away from the emergency room. She would tell me how she did it. You wouldn't believe the stories.'

'She would physically abuse herself? Like, cutting?'

'Cutting is different. Don't conflate the two.'

I tap my feet.

'With cutting, pain is the required effect. It's an emotional release. It's secretive. Munchausen is the opposite: Munchausens crave medical attention.'

'I find it difficult to believe that all of her injuries are self-inflicted. You haven't seen the state of her.

She was knocked out cold. Her teeth were broken, for Christ's sake.' A rotted picket fence.

'You need convincing. Have you seen her medical history? Decades of injuries.'

'In accordance with an abusive marriage.'

'Yes. Her syndrome does confound the usual scenario.'

'But she was honest with you?'

'I believe she craved attention from me as much as she did from the orthopaedics. And the plastic surgeons.'

'How do you know she was telling the truth? They're notorious deceivers, aren't they?'

'Aren't they, indeed,' he says.

I leave the psychiatrist's office, questions strumming my brain. Ignition, acceleration, autopilot.

'Why kill the husband?' Dom says. 'It doesn't fit with the diagnosis.'

'Shut up, Domino,' I say. 'This is real life. It's messy. Not everything is black and white. Not every psychological profile fits into a neat little box.'

'You're telling me,' he says, 'you're the one with the imaginary friend.'

'Is that what you are?' I say, adjusting the rearview mirror so that I can see him sitting upright on the back seat. He's wearing an especially handsome charcoal suit.

'I don't know what I am,' he says. 'I like to think of myself as a figment of your imagination. Figment. Fig-ment. It's a good word.'

'You're full of shit,' I say, moving the mirror back to its original position. Concentrating on the road.

'You do realise,' he says, 'that you've just insulted yourself.'

The Mini in front of me brakes suddenly and I almost smash into the back of it.

'I've got an idea,' I say. 'Let's drop the witty repertoire and talk about the suspect.'

'I *told* you she was the suspect,' Dom says.

'Is it just me, or is this case not making sense?'

'It's just you,' he says. 'Pretty cut and dried, as far as I can see. You're just hung up. On Her. As usual.' He yawns without bothering to cover his mouth.

'The husband's knuckles,' I say. 'They were bruised.'

'Yes,' says Dom. 'And the bedroom cupboards had holes in them. Maybe he was angry.'

I drum the steering wheel with my fingers. Not convinced.

'Okay, so … I'm going to give you another clue,' says Domino, as if indulging a particularly slow kid. 'Or, rather, I'm going to emphasise a detail you've already skipped over.'

I stop at a red light. I squint at him in the trembling mirror. 'I'm waiting.'

'What did you miss the first time around?'

'Everything, by the looks of it,' I say.

'Stop with the self-flagellation already.'

'Okay. We couldn't find the puzzle piece. The piece of the husband's skull.'

'RED HERRING!' Dom shouts right into my ear canal. 'What else?'

I think for a while. There was something bothering me. It was her teeth. Why do I keep thinking about her broken teeth?

'BINGO!' he shouts. 'Her chompers. Her pearly whites. Her rotten picket fence.'

'What do her teeth have to do with anything?'

'You want me to spell it out for you?'

God, I can be a bastard.

'Yes, I want you to spell it out for me.'

'I admit, it's left-field.'

'Just get on with it,' I say. I feel like I'm driving in circles.

'Remember that hippie girl you used to date. Brenda.'

Of course I remembered Brenda. Long straight hair. Honey breath. Hazelnut nipples.

'She used to analyse your dreams, right?' says Domino.

'This had better be going somewhere.'

'And you dreamt that weird tooth dream. Where you were keeping all your extra teeth in a tooth mug.'

'I vaguely recollect it.'

'And what did she tell you that was about?'

'Money. It was about money.'

'It was about money,' says Dom. 'What is the supposed root of all evil?'

'Money?'

'Money,' says Dom.

'Not some rare form of Munchausens?'

'Ha,' says Domino.

'But why the long story? Why lead the psychiatrist down the garden path? Why tell half-truths?'

'She had to tell someone something. She's human, after all. We all spin our own stories.'

I sigh.

'Really?' I say, 'Money?'

'Money, money, money,' says Domino. 'Show me the money. Hit me in the moneymaker. Skip to the money shot.'

'I get it.'

'Do you?'

'I do. She did it for the money.'

A couple of calls regarding the husband's bank account confirms the theory. Not that she needed it. She was wealthier than he was.

'I can't believe my deep gut / balls combination let me down,' I say.

'It didn't,' says Dom. 'It said she did it. It just didn't tell you the whole story.'

I picture the housecoat; this time stained with blood.

'Already a multi-millionaire before she met him,' I say. 'She's never had a job in her life. How does that work? Trust fund kid?'

Dom has decided he's helped me enough for the day. He left the back seat while I wasn't looking.

No, I think. No. She's this wealthy because she's done this before. And she got away with it. Over the past 12 years, two large previous payments to her account. Both hefty estates. Who would prosecute a battered wife? She's done this before. She's done it before, and she'll do it again. Third time lucky? Not if I can help it.

I jam my foot down. The accelerator touches the floor. I rush past hooting cars. One vehicle in particular reminds me of the fat black flies from this morning: A Peugeot with tinted windows buzzes around me until I shake it off. When I get to the hospital I drive straight through the parking boom and park in the emergency drop-off zone. I run up the stairs to the private wards and bust down her door. Her bed is empty. Her stuff is gone.

'Where is she?' I yell at the nurse — the one I had given a hard time.

'Gone,' he says. 'Checked herself out against doctors' orders. We haven't even had time to process the paperwork. She took her IV with. Still attached. Strung it up in her hired Peugeot.'

The nurse saunters away, trailing the cold fog of sanitiser.

'Son of a bitch,' I say.

He turns around. 'I knew she was faking something.'

7

GREY MAGIC

When people ask me what I do, I usually lie. I used to tell the truth, when I was young and had an exoskeleton woven from life-spirit and arrogance, as most young people do. Before that threaded shell was gradually eroded by the hurt in the world: the violence, the bad luck. Now only middle-aged, liver-spotted skin remains, which is no adequate barrier to life's bashing. Now I have to protect myself in other ways; age and wisdom bring another type of armour.

I used to tell the truth, but now the lies slide out of

my mouth like spotted eels. Easy and familiar. When I get bored of the untruths, I make up more, to keep things interesting. A year ago, I would have told you, if I had bumped into you at a conference or a cocktail party, that I was a botanist. The trick to believable deception, as I'm sure you know, is to keep it as truthful as possible. I have trained in botany, so it is an obvious one, one that springs quickly to my just-licked lips. But I am also qualified—fib-wise—to be a doctor, an astronomer, a zoologist, an archaeologist, a chemical engineer. Sometimes I surprise myself: my subconscious becomes adventurous, wants to pursue less lofty careers. I become a marketing consultant, a sous-chef, a yoga instructor.

When I was starting out, I thought I had to tell people what I did—what I really did—in order to get work, but I have since found that when you do the work well, the work will come. The universe, after all, supports action. Now, I only accept referrals from close friends and previous clients (the ones that are still alive, anyway).

The reality is there is never any shortage of demand for the kind of work I do. Telling strangers about my vocation hardly ever translates into real jobs, anyway. I find time-wasters incredibly annoying. I picture them as velcro-legged parasites that cling to my aura until they have unloaded their whole Sorry Story, only to refuse my offer of professional help. It takes all the self-control I can muster to not place some kind of small, irritating hex on them, a monkey on their back, just to cause them the same amount of chagrin that they have caused me. That kind of tit-for-tat may seem childish to you, but it keeps the cosmos nicely balanced. "An eye for an eye" out of the old book was never meant to be vengeful or malicious; it was instead to keep The Balance. If The Balance is off, bad things can happen. Some people call it karma, others say that "the wheel turns." It's all true, no matter how you choose to dress it up, with gory stories of biblical eye-gouging savagery or with glittering, ice-cream-coloured animal gods. The wheel just keeps on turning.

Worse than the time-wasters are the impromptu sermons delivered to me in inopportune places, like on the train, or standing in line for my daily fix. It's awkward. I'm always amazed at how many religious fanatics there are in our midst, dressed like ordinary people, slacks and crumpled tees, or polka-dotted summer dresses and glass beads, doing things that ordinary people do: eating processed-cheese sandwiches and listening to music on their phones. Using greasy hand cream that smells of roses. They seem so normal from the outside. It's only when they start babbling about necromantic prophets and being "saved" that you realise they have demons in their heads. When you look closely you see black scribbles on their auras. In my opinion, religious fundamentalism is a psychological disorder that has yet to be officially classified.

It's easy for me, in this day and age, to sit in the branches of my oak tree, feeling the light dapple my cheeks, the breeze lifting my hair, as if flying —when all feels right in the world—and ruminate about these people, but my predecessors weren't that lucky. There were no tree-dreams for them. No leisure to sit in a leafy bower and shine acorns, contemplating the spinning cycle of life.

Just a couple of hundred years ago I would have been dragged down and lit up. Sometimes I wake up in a fever, as if I am on fire. It spreads from my feet upwards, like I am burning on a stake somewhere in a parallel (or previous) life. The first time it happened, when I was a little girl, I just lay there and blazed. I remember feeling paralysed by the fear of my destiny; perhaps even wished to burn up altogether. Wished to be nothing more than a glint of sad ashes in the creeping morning light. The next day, my legs were covered in blisters. The time after that, I ran an ice bath as soon as I felt it start, which I have been doing ever since. I lie in the arctic water and listen to my heart slow: run ice cubes over my flickering skin, absorbing the cold; the opposite of a sun lizard. Sometimes the fever brings with it auditory hallucinations: chanting, shouting, the sound of an angry mob. The crackling of a spiteful fire. I don't know if I experience these episodes because my energy has an intense empathy for my foremothers, or if they are echoes of my previous, or future, lives. Whatever the reason, I thank the universe daily for the Age of Enlightenment. Of course, I use the word "enlightenment" loosely. I'm also grateful for my ice machine.

So I lie about what I do because of the fundamentalists and the time-wasters, and also to preserve my psychic energy. I've had enough of the rubber-necking. This fox mantle of dishonesty, this deception, can be lonely, but in my experience—and as parents warn—no good comes from talking to strangers.

At the moment, if anyone asks, I'm a shopkeeper. In a way it's true: I sell all kinds of ideas scratched on paper. I've always liked the idea of owning a bookshop.

It's not only strangers I lie to. I am less than honest with my clients, too. I guess you could say that I place less emphasis on the truth than most people, but only ever for the right reasons. I find honesty for the sake of honesty naïve and often unnecessarily harmful. Sometimes a profoundly dishonest act can have a major positive affect on someone's life. For example, a client of mine—let's call her "Betty"—was having trouble getting pregnant. I could sense, in the first consultation, that she was perfectly fertile (her energy was the colour of a ripe mandarin) but despite this, Betty's womb remained stubbornly barren. I told her I'd have her pregnant within three new moons. All it would take was some skillful spellcrafting, an eggshell sail, and a little resourcefulness on my side. In the Dark Ages we were called "the cunning folk" for good reason.

It was clear to me that her husband's sperm was the problem, although Betty wouldn't entertain this idea, wouldn't even "insult him" by having him tested, as if he was some kind of caveman with the emotional intelligence of a Sumatran Orangutan. The matter of their infertility was not even discussed in their household, apart from their monthly ritual of him shooting reproachful looks at her tear-stained face, raw and bruised by her steady disappointment.

They had been trying for six years, which was good news for me: 6 is an incredibly fertile number, as you can probably guess from the shape. It also told me that if it hadn't happened by now, it probably wasn't going to happen unless I took some drastic action.

Once I was prepared, Betty was mid-cycle, and the moon was full, it was time to cast the spell. She had invited her sister, Danielle, for moral support, as she was keeping my services a secret from her Orangutan.

"I just want you to know that I don't approve of what you do," were the first words the sister said to me.

"Okay," I said, and continued to unpack my things. I would have preferred "Hello."

"I just don't think it's right," she insisted.

"Oh, Danielle," sighed Betty.

"In fact, I think…" she started. I could tell that she was about to hit her stride if I didn't interrupt her.

"You are more than welcome," I said, "to wait outside."

"Out-side?" she said, as if it was the first time she had ever heard the word. I found myself wishing that she would close her gaping-fish mouth. If we were characters in a comic book I could have waved my wand—abracadabra!—and turned her into a puffer fish, bouncing and flapping on the kitchen floor.

"There is no place for negative energy here tonight," I said, slowly and clearly, to the sister. "If you have a problem, it's best to go, and leave this sacred space." I was hamming it up a bit, for effect. Perhaps I am less mature than I give myself credit for.

"Sacred?" she gasped. "Sacred?" It took remarkable restraint on my behalf to not ask her if English was her first language. If her reaction wasn't interfering with my work I would have found her outrage quite entertaining.

"Look, Dan, this was a mistake."

"Yes! That's what I was trying to tell you!"

"No, I mean, I think you should go," Betty said to her, gently.

"I'm not leaving you with this…this…"

What would she think would happen if she left her sister in my supposedly evil clutches, I wondered? That I would possess her, kill her, steal her soul? I wasn't surprised by Danielle's attitude. You are bound to bump up against some people in my business, people who believe that witchery is wicked. Little do they know that they cast spells themselves, when they curse other drivers in traffic, touch wood, or blow out birthday candles.

"I need this to work," said Betty.

"Listen to me," whispered her sister, bunching up her fists around the gold crucifix that dangled from her moist and unpleasantly chunky neck. "You don't need to do this. Come to our church! Our cell group has been praying for you…"

"And she has yet to conceive," I said. "You say you don't like spells, what do you think prayer is? You just haven't been saying the right ones."

Blasphemy! her aura shouted.

"And I suppose you know the right ones?" She eyed me: a wolf in wolf's clothing.

"Yes," I said. "It's my job."

I began the ceremony by smudging the room with the sweet smoke of lavender and white sage. With a piece of chalkstone I drew a circle on the pine floorboards around Betty, on which I placed six green candles. I anointed the candles with vanilla oil, lit them, then began my fertility incantation. Betty was instructed to close her eyes and sit as still as possible, as if meditating, and just allow the spell to wash through her. Her hands were placed over her abdomen, sending warmth and acceptance deep into her pelvic chakra. Afterwards, we sailed the eggshell by moonlight while Betty recited a poem she had written, inviting the soul of her baby into her body. I found her vulnerability touching, and couldn't help thinking that she would make a tender mother. I gave her a silver bracelet with a charm of a carnelian-eyed hare—I had charged the crystal with pentacle-cast spells—as well as a gift of bespoke tea: stinging nettle, red clove and raspberry leaf, which she was to drink every day. She held my hands and thanked me. On my way out, I gave her a syringe I had been keeping warm between my breasts. I told her it was a potion to open and soften her cervix, and that she should keep it at blood temperature and use it before making love to her husband that night.

Six weeks later, Betty was pregnant, as I knew she would be. She has since given birth to a bonny little boy with a full head of hair and an easy smile. Her Orangutan will never know that the child is not biologically his.

The timing of Betty's lunacycle couldn't have been more perfect. I had been consulting that day with another client of mine who was having trouble sustaining his phallus. Feri, or sexual mysticism, is a speciality of mine, and I had been training him in the art of Tantra. This client wasn't dissimilar-looking to the man in the wedding photo that Betty had given me. Without going into too many details, this client had inadvertently given me the means to help Betty. The universe had been particularly supportive that day, as it can be, when you are following a beneficent course of action. Neither client was aware of the transaction, and they were both extremely pleased with the results. Had I been honest with either of them, the outcome would not have been nearly as satisfactory.

The thing about earth magic is that it can go either way. We are all under the influence of so many factors at any one time that it's not an exaggeration to say that anything can happen. Without even knowing it, our destinies are pushed and pulled by the sparkling cosmos, kneaded and knocked back like baker's dough. You can try your best to stake out your life's path—or others' lives, as I do—but our human influence is limited. There are people—women and men—who become taken with a neo-pagan lifestyle, study Wicca, indulgently call themselves White Witches. But if they truly knew their craft, they would know that there is no such thing. These dabblers are the moths of the sorcery world, not unpleasant to have around, unless they get confused and start battering themselves against a light-source that is not the moon. Some are elegant and pretty to look at, others leave moth-dust and holes in your winter underwear.

There is no such thing as white magic. Real magic is a wide spectrum encompassing good and evil, and there are very many shades of grey in-between. The reason a spell can never be pure white is because of the cosmic baker's influence. A sorceress may start out with a clear, benevolent purpose, unalloyed ingredients, and a pure heart, and perform the incantation as close to perfect as she can manage, but after that, she has little influence. Once it is out of her mouth, the spell is out of her hands, and cannot be kept un-grubby.

As with magic, is with witches. Just as a person cannot be 100 percent good, a witch, as pure-thinking as she may be, cannot achieve Perfect Snow. Witches are human, after all. She may be milk, ivory, or limestone, or one of the hundreds of shades between them, but never fresh snow. You have this trembling human spectrum overlapping and interweaving with the sure orbit of magic, and it becomes evident—despite the illusions of the giggling Wiccans—that a White Witch is nothing but a fairytale.

I am under none of the pagan pretences. I practice grey magic; more dove-grey than charcoal. Or more accurately: the colour of a raincloud as it swells and shrinks and flickers between shades of pearl and slate. I have to be careful of slipping to-wards the sooty part of the spectrum. The darker the magic, the quicker the flame takes, the more powerful you feel. You have to be on your guard and think things through: sometimes you set out to do good and the result is murky, or worse. I once killed someone with a simple love spell. That may sound like I'm just not a very proficient witch, but the opposite is true. The spell was one of my best: refined over and over again to be as simple and striking as possible. But setting out, I wasn't told the whole story. A woman had left a man, and the spell was to reunite them. What I hadn't been told was that the woman had left the man for someone else. That someone else happened to meet with an accident the day I triple-cast the reunion conjuration: an innocent bystander, he was shot in a cash-in-transit heist. My client, his grief-stricken lover returned, had been delighted, and paid me double. It had not been my intention. Apparently they are happily married now. He still sends me fruit baskets.

Taking lives is not always dark sorcery. Counterintuitive as it may seem, killing people is sometimes the kindest, and most important work I do. In a topsy-turvy society such as ours, where your life is not your own, a sensible outsider—not bound by popular morality—is sometimes required. On occasion, a client needs to be supported in their decision to perform certain actions that are usually frowned upon by the bleating world at large. This is where my services come in, as a non-judgmental advisor, helper, sponsor, drug dealer, psychologist, relationship counsellor, prostitute, or mercy nurse. Being a witch isn't about spells and trickery—not really—more than anything else, it's about having a completely open mindset, and having the courage of your convictions. In short, to be a consummate witch, you have to have a titanium spine.

I help the client take a psychic step away from their supposed reality, and offer them a perspective that is unconstrained by the values of others. I coax them out of the dogma-box. Although most people seem happy to be trained and controlled by banks, employers and television, it is only when we are unfettered by indoctrination that we can live our free and true lives. I help people with this awakening, but often this bitter-bright truth comes too late, when they are in an acute crisis, or are dying.

The client I am busy working with has stage 4 pancreatic cancer. He joked when he called me, saying: "there is no stage 5". He needed someone who was willing to end his life for him, when the time came, and he found that time rapidly approaching. Just a month ago, he told me, he was driving his Porsche Carrera with the top down, meeting friends for lunch, drinking Scotch, and following the Premier League. But now he finds his appetite vanished, his balance is off. He can't hear properly, doesn't have the energy to drive.

"Could it be true?" he asks me, "That my drive to the café around the corner, for the paper, was my last? That I'll never drive again?"

It wasn't just his beloved car he was grieving for, of course, but his independence. His life as he knew it. He is plagued by a constant "empty" pain in his abdomen that gnaws at his mood. He has no children, his wives are all estranged. His doctor says her hands are tied, there are no more treatments available, that she can only make him "comfortable."

"Comfortable?" he demands. "What the hell is comfortable about dying?"

I wouldn't say he is at peace with his impending death, but he doesn't want to live like this. Not when we know there will be no improvement.

"I should be grateful, I suppose," he says to me, "Going downhill so quickly. It's what every terminal patient hopes for...once you reach the top of the hill, that is."

It's difficult to be grateful when you feel your life is being snatched away. He is not the kind of man who will accept being bedridden, or fed chicken broth with a spoon. He has lost 8 kg in the past two weeks. When he can no longer walk, I take things to cheer him up. He still likes iced coffee but refuses berry pinwheel pastries, his former favourite combination.

On the third day, the heavens open up and blast us with a dramatic thunderstorm. Once the rain slows I follow the sound of mewling outside to discover trees stripped by wind and a skinny-ribbed kitten with opalescent eyes. I rub her dry with a tea towel to reveal tiger stripes and chinchilla-soft fur. I place her on my client's chest, and she soothes him with her loud purring.

I read the newspaper to him as his consciousness swims in and out of shallow sleep. I tell him the soccer score, who has saved a goal, who has been carded. I am with him for five days and five nights. Every hour drains me, although I try not to show it. We do this pretend-dance of patient and nurse until today when he takes my wrist in his cool bony fingers and says he is ready.

The truth is that nothing is being snatched away from him, not permanently. Once his heart stops knocking and his cells power down, his energy will move on to a better place. Not heaven (or hell), not a resting place, but a living place. I have told him that energy cannot be destroyed, only converted, but his imagination cannot stretch that far. It's not a "better place"—not necessarily, just different—like a new day. You don't know exactly what it will hold, but it will surely be kinder to him than this suffering. We are all souls surfing through history. This moving on, this energy conversion, is why I have no problem with ending someone's current life. It is no more sinister than putting a child to sleep.

There is a common misconception that ending a terminal illness requires active euthanasia, but this is most often not the case. The majority of the time, all that is needed is for the patient to sign a living will that refuses any further medical treatment, and for the caregivers to respect his or her wishes. The very last thing a terminally ill patient wants is to be fussed over with antibiotics and feeding tubes in order to prolong his pain, but this is often what families insist on. They panic and press red buttons and jam oxygen masks over their loved ones' faces, despite their clear DNR stickers, because they are the ones afraid of death.

In most cases I have found that if you cut off all access to medical treatment and are liberal with the painkillers, nature takes its course easily, and the soul is allowed to ascend, un-barbed, to its beckoning place. Sometimes gentle help is needed: extra analgesics, if you can get them, or a steady pillow over a slumbering face.

"I'm ready," he says to me now, clear-eyed. "I'm ready to go."

With a long match, I light the nine black candles in the room, and smudge with sandalwood and willow. I put a smooth Obsidian stone in his palm. I recite the Druidic Death Hex under my breath. The kitten's purring gets louder as the magic electrifies the room. I load up a syringe with morphine, nine times the prescribed dose, and push the needle into one of the beetroot-purple veins that snake over his arms. I can see the effects of the drug cascade over him; his relief is instant. I hold his hand as the spirit leaves his body. I feel a pull, a falling away, and then it's gone. The room exhales. The wheel turns, the cycle spins. There is no need to check his pulse, or put a mirror near his mouth to search for breath. Nothing remains but a sad skeleton in skin. The kitten cries.

I blow out the candles and pack my things, including a fat envelope of cash with my name on it. I wipe the house down to vanish any fingerprints. After a moment's hesitation, I put the moping kitten in my basket, too. I have always resisted having a cat, given my occupation. It seemed a terrible cliché, like sporting a wart on my nose, or flying a broom.

Today, however, I no longer mind the idea. I let myself out of the house, and leave the polished key under the doormat. The wind has picked up, and dead leaves flutter and swirl across my path like ugly butterflies. The moon is waning, and I'm feeling a bit older, colder, bashed-about.

Burnt out. Ashes to glinting ashes.

It will be nice to have a warm creature at home. We can sit in the oak tree together.

8

PIGEON PAIR

"They're quite pretty things, really," says Juliet.

Edward, intent on smoothing the marmalade on his cold toast in exactly the right way, doesn't hear — or ignores her — and she has to wave at him to break his trance.

"This one isn't quite as good as the thick cut, but it IS easier to spread," he says.

The pair of pigeons coo. It's a gentle, happy sound. Their swivelling necks are iridescent.

"Quite nice to have some birds around," she says.

"The colour is good. You want that golden hue, don't you? You want those strips of blood orange and pink grapefruit. You want that syrupy sheen."

"Edward," says Juliet.

"It's a most underrated condiment, I think. Sweet, with just the right amount of bitterness. And that tang — that citrus tang ..."

"Edward! Will you snap out of it?"

Coo! Coo! say the pigeons, beady black eyes watching the couple at the table below.

"What?" he says at last, dragging his eyes off the jar and looking at her. "Did I miss something?"

Sometimes Juliet thinks that she may as well eat breakfast on her own, for all the attention she gets from her husband. Sometimes she would say something — just something small — to make con-versation, and he would flat-out ignore her. Not an acknowledging glance, not a mumble of agreement.

"I was just saying that the pigeons are quite pretty. I don't know why they have such a bad reputation."

"Do they?" he asks, taking a bite of his vaunted toast. "Do they have a bad reputation?"

He crunches and grinds the toast in his mouth. Juliet has to talk over the sound or she fixates on it. She hates hearing people chew. Apparently there is a scientific name for it. It's an actual condition. It drives her crazy.

"Yes. People call them vermin," she says.

In the past she had asked him to try to make less noise while eating, and he had flung his head back and laughed. How? He had asked. How does one do that? Even if I wanted to indulge this particular eccentricity of yours. How does one chew quietly?

She had not mentioned it again. He takes another bite and crunch, crunch, crunch, like a car compactor. Like a bone breaking. Like stepping on crushed glass.

"Vermin?" he says. "That seems extreme."

"Yes," she says, "I agree," and she does.

Misophonia, it's called. She read about it in a magazine. The irrational anger one feels upon hearing others eat. At least she wasn't the only one. His mouth must feel so dry with all that toast and sugar, she thinks. Doesn't he want some water?

"Would you like some water?" she asks, lifting the glass jug. It drips with condensation. He doesn't answer. She pours it anyway.

The pigeons, having had enough of the breakfast show, launch themselves with a clatter of wings off the boundary wall and into the bright sky. The Bentworths watch them fly away.

"Anyway, you know that we need to stop buying that particular underrated condiment," says Juliet.

"This?" he says, showing her his last golden square. "Sacrilege! Why would you say that?"

"It's full of sugar," she says. "You know what your doctor said."

"Oh, please," he says. "I've been eating sugar my whole life and look at me!" He beats his chest, Tarzan-like. "I'm as healthy as an ox!"

"Not according to Doctor Benson, you're not," she says. "And I don't want you to get diabetes."

Edward grunts and looks away. Rinses his mouth with a sip of cold tea. Juliet picks up the offending jar.

"We shouldn't be buying this anyway," Juliet says. "It's imported from Paris!"

"So?" he says. "That's what makes it good!"

"No," says Juliet. "Its irresponsible."

"It's organic!"

"It's reckless."

"Ha!" he says. "Now I've heard it all."

"It's true," says Juliet. "Think of our trade deficit. We should really be buying local."

"So our pretty birds are vermin, hey?" says Edward. "And now marmalade is reckless. Now I've really heard it all."

"Shall I give them some of these toast crumbs?"

"Don't you dare."

"Why aren't you dressed yet?" asks Edward. He is

wearing his tuxedo and is looking especially hand-some. Steam is still pouring out of the en-suite. There's probably no hot water left.

"Why am I not dressed yet?" Juliet says, looking down at her tracksuit pants stained with puréed butternut and crusted with bright blue bubblefruit toddler toothpaste. "Are you serious?"

While Edward had skipped home from work and jumped right into the shower, Juliet had been wrangling the children. Emma had to be fed her baby slop, and topped up with milk. Dean needed fish fingers and peas, which was more of a theoret-ical exercise in eating than actual eating, seeing as they all landed up on the floor. Juliet had given up and made him two-minute noodles with tomato sauce for what was now the third night in a row. Then they both needed to be bathed and dressed and made ready for bed, which was always an exer-cise in patience and steel determination, especially with the one-parent to two-kid ratio. The saying about herding cats always came to mind, but a glance at Laila, the family cat, snoozing peacefully on the couch made Juliet feel that herding cats would certainly be easier. A bit of smelly tuna and shaking some kibble in a bowl would probably do the trick. The kids — her kids — her home-made gremlins, required considerably more effort.

"Where's the babysitter?" he says, angling his chin up to the ceiling and looking in the mirror to inspect his freshly shaven throat.

"She'll be here at 7."

He shakes his watch down his arm and looks at the face. Picks up his phone, ready to check the Premier League results.

"You can make their milk and go in and read them a story," says Juliet, taking off her stained cardigan, "while I make myself presentable."

"It had better be a long story," he says, winking at her.

She throws her top at him. It hits him square in the face and he catches it as it falls.

"Oh," she says. "Before I forget. The pigeons are back."

"Are they?"

"And they brought a few friends with them."

"Is it a problem?"

"I don't think so. They're entertaining, anyway, for the kids. I showed Dean how to shoo them away and it keeps him occupied for ages."

Edward shakes Juliet awake. She opens her eyes but sees nothing.

"What's wrong?" she says, heart-in-throat. *Is something wrong with one of the kids? Has someone broken in? Why didn't the house alarm go off?*

"Can you hear them?" he demands.

Juliet tries to listen but all she can hear is her pulse banging in her ears.

"What?"

"It's the birds. It's those bloody birds."

"A dream?" wonders Juliet out loud.

"You can't hear them? It's like they've nested right next to my head! I can't sleep with them making such a racket."

Juliet hears them. Enthusiastic cooing; wing adjusting; sharp claws grubbing on tin.

"I can hear them," she says. She looks at her phone: 4:30AM. "Looks like we have ourselves a new alarm clock."

"Mama?" says Dean, sleep-walking into the bedroom. She jumps out of bed and swoops to catch him before he tumbles down the two stairs. Brings his warm body into bed with them. Kisses his head.

Coo! Coo! say the birds.

"Ed? You there?" says Juliet into he receiver. "Ed?"

"I'm just walking into a meeting. It's been a hell of a day so far. Can we chat later?"

"It's the pigeons!"

"You're calling me because of the … pigeons?"

"They've made such a mess. There's just … there's just feathers and sticks and bird shit everywhere!

All over the outside furniture. The settee, the shelves, the flat screen!"

"Can't you just, you know, shoo them away?"

"Shoo them away? There are like, 20 of them."

"Didn't you say that Dean loved chasing them away?"

"He does! He does it all day! It's practically his part-time job. He's not even 2!"

"You said it was cute."

"It used to be cute. He puts his arms up and stomps on the floor — like a gumboot dance — very effective — but even he can't keep up with the way they're flocking in here."

"Let me go in to this meeting. I'll try get back as soon as I can."

"Hmm," says the man in the bright yellow overall. "Hmm."

He sucks his pencil and narrows his eyes and inspects the eaves where the pigeons have been nest-ing. Dirty patches on white timber trusses where bird feet have been dancing the cha-cha. He makes some notes.

"I can see they've already caused some damage," he says, eyeing the flatscreen TV with a disapproving look.

"I probably should have called you sooner," says Juliet.

"Hmm," the man says.

The timber floor decking underneath the eaves is an abstract painting. Jackson Pollock in guano. The yellow man sniffs. He does not appreciate the artistic merit. The logo on his overall is the same as the picture on his van: a cheerful looking pigeon holding a suitcase and saluting, as if he is leaving for a quick island holiday. As if these yellow men are really travel agents for burnt-out birds.

"Nine THOUSAND rand?" says Edward, hitting a button on his keyboard over and over again, as if to correct a mistake.

"I know!" says Juliet. "It's ridiculous."

"Are you sure they didn't send us the wrong quote?" he says, hand over brow.

"It's the netting that's expensive. And the spikes. And the labour."

"Netting AND spikes? Is that really necessary? I don't want all this stuff cluttering our space. I spent a fortune on that outside area. I don't want it to look like we're living in bloody Fort Knox!"

It does sometimes feel like a prison, thinks Juliet.

"Is there no other way?"

"I don't know. It does seem excessive."

"Nine thousand rand?"

"He did seem to know what he was talking about."

"Can't we find a way to chase them away, ourselves?"

"I've tried!"

Juliet had dug around in the kids' playroom and

found a rubber snake, which she had placed in the birds' favourite spot. They just shat on it.

"They just shit on it," she says, tugging a strand of her hair. "They just shit on everything!"

Edward was used to compliments on his house. They used to please him.

"My God," says his sister, almost losing her grip on her glass of wine before she'd had a sip. "What on earth is going on here?"

"You wouldn't believe it," says Juliet, bouncing baby Emma on her hip. "I've become a guerrilla."

"What the —" she says, trailing off, taking in the odd new decorations. Usually she was proud of the fact that the Bentworths had exceptional taste, but —

"The old CDs hanging like that," says Juliet, "like 80s bunting, is to keep them away. The sun reflects off them and disorients them."

"Disorientates who?" says Sarah.

"You don't know?"

"Know about what?"

"Our problem!" says Juliet.

"We have a feral pigeon problem," says Edward.

"I've put tinfoil on all the surfaces," says Juliet.

"I can see that," says Sarah.

"I chase them with a broom. I throw balls at them. They're so bloody stupid and so stubborn … sometimes I get so angry I just wish I had a pellet gun!"

"Now THAT'S a good idea," says Edward.

"And I placed fake eggs everywhere. You know, because Google said that they won't nest in another bird's nest. Poor Dean got so excited. He thought we were going to have an Easter egg hunt!"

A pigeon dives in, dodges the CDs and lands on the tinfoil. Emma starts wailing. Juliet get tears in her eyes.

"Juliet? Are you okay?"

"No," says Juliet. "No, I'm not."

Sarah, not good at comforting people, puts her glass down and gives Juliet an awkward hug. Pats the baby.

"You poor thing," she says. "Don't worry. We'll sort these bloody birds out."

A group of men in yellow overalls swarm all over the deck. Ladders are employed; nail guns shoot their columns of steel into the wood with a satisfying bang. Strong black netting is rolled out: the opposite of a red carpet.

"Bird eviction, they call it," says Edward, looking cheerful despite not having slept well in days. "I find that quite funny."

Before their eyes, their minimalist and tastefully decorated outside area becomes a crazy quilt of pigeon prophylactics. Ligatures, gauze, spikes.

"Once the birds have been dispatched," says Edward to the yellow chief (the man who sucks the pencil), "Can we get all this removed?"

Juliet sees the timber trusses being punctured. Penetrated. Perforated. Even if they remove the unwelcome deterrents, the deck will remain scarred.

"Sure you can," says the man. "If you want them to come back."

Edward pays him ten thousand rand.

That evening Edward and Juliet deposit the children in front of the television and drink an aperitif outside, trying to ignore the unsightly eviction gear. They want to see the pigeons swoop in and realise there is nowhere for them to nest. They want to see them get frustrated and fly away. The Bentworths have never considered themselves cruel people but as they sip their scotches in silence all they wish for is to see the pigeons lose hope. They wish for pigeon doom and despair. They swallow their drinks. The birds don't come.

"Do you think it was enough to scare them away?" asks Juliet, as they lie in bed. She wishes he would hold her hand. When was the last time they held hands? "The army of yellow men, I mean. Do you think the pigeons recognised them and just knew not to come back?"

"Maybe," said Edward, yawning. "He did say that he does a lot of work in the area."

"So we've just chased them to some other unfortunate person's house."

Emma fusses in the cot next to their bed, but settles down without reassurance.

"Maybe, in future, we won't need all that terrible netting," says Juliet. "Maybe we can fill the holes and repaint."

She waits for a reply but Edward is asleep. She leans over him to switch off his bedside light.

Juliet stirs: woken by the scratching. Pins on sheet metal. Before she is even properly awake she knows the pigeons are back. How is that possible? she thinks. How the bloody hell is that possible?

She gets up quietly as to not wake Edward or the baby. Fetches Dean's alligator torchlight, but not before stepping on a piece of Lego and gulping down a string of curses. Uses her remote to switch off the house alarm, but forgets the outside beams. She pads to the back door that leads to the deck, unlocks it, steps down into the cool dark breeze.

Sweeps the toy light over the eaves which are free of birds, checks the furniture; the flatscreen. The shadows are still and quiet.

Had she imagined it? Had it been a dream? There was certainly no evidence of trespassers here. But then there is a flicker in her peripheral vision, which makes her jump. What — she thinks, and then she sees it. A pigeon on her clean white shelf: hiding. Playing dead? Juliet runs towards it to shoo it away, and it gets such a fright it explodes in a clatter of wings and feathers, knocking a flower vase off the shelf, which falls and shatters on the floor. The sound is jarring in the otherwise silent morning. The bird, discombobulated, flies into the wall, then finds his way out. His pitching signals the security beams and sets off the alarm: the siren caterwauls all around her. Emma and Dean are both startled awake and start crying. They both want her but she is sweeping up the shards to pro-tect their tender little feet. Edward tries to hold them back, and then his phone starts ringing, adding to the cacophony. He assures the security company that it was a false alarm. The armed men arrive anyway. The control room had sensed he had been acting under duress.

"Coffee," says Juliet.

"Is that an offer, or a demand?" asks Edward.

"Here." She puts a double shot espresso in his hand. He takes a sip.

"Oh, this is good. What did I do to deserve you?"

"I'm not sure you do deserve me," Juliet says. He knows she is not joking.

"I'm taking the day off," he says, draining his cup. His eyes are red, puffy. He hasn't shaved in a couple of days. He's looking quite grey.

"Are you that tired?"

Despite his demeanor of exhaustion, there is a sparkle in his eyes.

"It's not that," says Edward. "I'm going to camp out on the deck. I'm going to make sure that those damned pigeons don't come back."

"Really?" says Juliet, warming to him. "Maybe you do deserve me after all."

While Juliet takes the kids to the park, Edward goes shopping to buy supplies for his mission. They rendezvous back at the house. Edward is wearing a new, lightweight camouflage jacket, and beige pants. He looks like a fly fisherman, or an army vet. There are black smudges under his eyes. Had he used her eye-liner? She pulls on her bush outfit: khaki 3-phase zipper pants and a tan blouse. She wipes off her red lipstick and goes with a nude shade instead. Looks in the mirror: feels decidedly German. She joins him out on the deck, puts a thermos flask and Dean's dinosaur-themed tin lunchbox on the table in front of him.

"Sandwiches," she says. "And tea."

Edward nods in approval. Wonders offhandedly what is on the sandwiches.

The provisions she has brought sit in contrast with the weapons on the table: a pneumatic pellet gun, with plenty of pretty copper-coloured BBs. A BirdX Quadblaster QB4, which, according to the box, repelled pigeons with its ultrasonic waves. A

Broadband Ray with Fright Visuals. A Nightmare Sound 4-Speaker. A plastic 'action owl' decoy with a movement sensor. He had already planted the additional spikes he had bought: on the handrail, on the lemon tree, on every inch of open shelf. Her decorative porcelain rabbits and cats now sat behind an aggressive row of metal skewers.

She watches as he loads the air gun. "You're really going to shoot them?" she says.

"Yip," he says, flicking the safety catch off and looking through the rifle's sight. It makes her nervous.

"Be careful of Laila," she says. "Don't shoot her."

"What use is a cat if it doesn't catch the pigeons?" he says. She smacks him on the arm and the gun almost goes off. He forgets to put the safety back on.

"I don't blame Laila," says Juliet. "Would you want a mouthful of vermin?"

"That's a good point," he says. "The cat's a Bentworth, after all. I daresay that a dirty pigeon is quite beneath her station."

Edward installs the various kits he has bought. Juliet assists him: holding ladders, passing screwdrivers, finding extension cables for the electric drill. As she sweeps up after him she can't help noticing how much damage the birds have done. Their acidic droppings have corroded almost every surface she sees. She imagines her precious things covered in diseases and lice. Suddenly she has to drop everything to viciously scratch her head.

"Pigeon lice," she says, scrubbing away. "I'm sure I'm imagining it."

Edward shudders in empathy.

Eventually they are all set up. The deck is unrecognisable, strewn with cables and lights and panels.

"I like the fake owl," Juliet says. "Let's keep him after the pigeons are gone."

"Watch this," says Edward. He runs up to the owl and waves at it. The owl screeches and his head swivels. His eyes are red lasers.

"My God," she says. "That's enough to give anyone nightmares."

Edward chuckles. "Isn't it wonderful?"

He flaps his arms again and the owl responds. It reminds Juliet of the film 'The Exorcist.' Edward keeps laughing.

They send the kids to their Aunt Sarah for the afternoon while they sit in their camping chairs drinking gin & tonics and eating kettle-fried chips. Laila has forgiven Edward, as evidenced by her sleeping on his lap.

"Look at us," says Juliet. If it wasn't the middle of summer they could have matching blankets on their knees. "Sitting here like an old couple."

"We ARE an old couple," says Edward, looking through his binoculars at some birds in the distance.

Juliet thinks he is looking quite handsome, despite his grey stubble.

"We're probably wasting our time," says Juliet. "I mean, there's no way they're coming back now, with all these gadgets."

"Never say never."

Juliet has her iPad and is reading up on feral pigeons. When she finds something interesting she reads it out loud. "Did you know that they don't migrate?"

"Ha," says Edward, pursing his lips. "Just our luck."

"Did you know that they are monogamous?"

"Are they?"

"You only think of lovely, elegant animals being monogamous, don't you? Swans, for instance. Wolves."

"What's that?" says Edward, sitting up straight.

"I was just saying …"

"Sshhh!" he says, putting a finger to his lips. "What's that sound?"

Juliet listens. There is a murmuring. A distinct pigeon cooing, coming from the roof. They abandon their drinks and scuttle over to the sound.

"There's a pigeon in there," he says. "Inside the bloody roof."

"More than one!" she says. "But how did they get in?"

"I don't care. I'm going to take them out." Edward drags the ladder to the offending area and scrambles up. Juliet hold the ladder still. She hears "Ah - ha!" as he finds their hiding place behind a loose brick.

She wants to call up: Be Careful, but Edward hates it when she says that, so she keeps quiet instead. He forces out the brick and hits the wall next to it to dislodge any feathered vagrants.

Neither of them are prepared for the swarm of birds that erupt from the opening. One hundred, two hundred pigeons, moving together, like an animated, monstrous mass. The fake owl screeches; Laila bolts. The horde flies around and then descend on the deck, on the shelves, on the flatscreen, on the camping chairs, on Juliet and Edward. Everything is covered in twitching grey wings and black-pearl eyes. The Bentworths scream and bat the birds away. Claws scrabble at their skin. Edward's face turns white and he grabs his chest.

Juliet runs towards the pellet gun. The owl

screeches again, sending a wave of birds up into the air, and Juliet shoots six birds in a row, without missing. Edward, slightly recovered, picks up Dean's nearby water pistol and starts shooting, too. The BirdX Quadblaster is sending out ultrasonic waves that make the ground vibrate. Juliet kills another five birds, which sends half the flock skittering off. Three more birds with pellets in their hearts fall to the floor, and with the soft, wet smack of the third's body hitting the timber, the rest of the legion wing themselves away. Downy feathers rain like snow down around them.

Juliet and Edward sit together amongst the carcasses and lost plumes. Juliet has ribbons of fresh blood on her cheek where she had been scratched. She doesn't put down the rifle. Edward is still pale, and he has bird shit on the shoulder of his camo jacket. The sun is beginning to set. They look at each other.

"I thought you were having a heart attack," she says.

"Me too," he says. "But it's over now."

"I don't think they're coming back," she says.

"They are definitely NOT coming back," he says. "You made sure of that."

Edward reaches over, and they hold hands.

In the distance, on someone else's property, a pair of pigeons coo and settle in for the night.

9

THE LITTLE PINK BOOK

H er scream smashes the ceiling. It knocks over a vase of blue chrysanthemums, whips out of the room and into the corridor, bowling over nurses as it goes. It is eardrum-popping, eye-watering, and desolate.

Sister Angelika's disembodied head appears at the doorway. Jesus.

"Is everything alright in here?" she demands, jowls aquiver.

"Yes, Sister." My rubber soles squeak innocence.

"But what is all this noise about? I could hear the bawling from the chapel!"

My smile is glacé. I mop up the spilt water from the fallen flowers.

"Well," I venture, "this is a maternity ward."

Sister Angelika's eyes disappear and reappear in an extravagant show of blinking. I put my hands on my hips.

"A baby's head's circumference is usually around thirty-five centimetres," I add, in case she didn't quite get the point.

An apoplectic jump.

"Well, it's upsetting the geriatrics. They're all in a flurry! They can't hear the television and now they're refusing to take their meds! Could you at least make an effort to keep it down?"

"Oh, of course," I say, "by all means. God bless the geriatrics."

A departing sniff and she is gone.

I take my patient's wrist to measure her pulse against my wristwatch. I wink at her.

"Let's see if you can scream any louder."

Sister Angelika detests midwives. She thinks of us as unnatural. The irony of that, I'm sure, escapes her. I think the whole idea of reproduction escapes her. I can imagine her nose stinging at the thought of it. The steamy interchanging of bodily fluids, the milk-swelling of breasts, the gush of water, the inky blood. Immaculate conception is far more her cup of holy water. If she were residing over a birth the patient would probably be told to lie still, stay quiet and keep her legs crossed. Bless the Catholics.

My patient, Miss June Catrilby, is a lovely woman. (Yes! *Miss!* Sister Angelika would be throwing her frown around if only she knew that an illegitimate baby was causing all this fuss). June and I got along right away. It's critical that an expectant mother likes and trusts her midwife. When one is in such a vulnerable position one needs to be in the company of only those she trusts. We'll have a doctor on standby, and an attending nurse, but for the most part it will be June and I doing the work.

June told me that the father of the baby ran away, seemingly without a backward glance. June didn't seem too bothered about it; said that they'd be better off without him. He's probably married. Or worse - in politics. I am by no stretch of the imagination a moralist, but I do believe that a child needs a father. At least June knows that I am here for her.

I wanted to be a surgeon but I failed my fifth year of med school. I was the only woman admitted to the medical faculty that year and I skipped eating and sleeping on most days to keep up with the workload until one day I just fell down in a practical exam. My psychologist at the time attributed it to burnout. I had put myself under too much pressure for too long: I was hospitalised for exhaustion. It was a relief. I stuck an IV drip in my arm and spent a few days sleeping. Every insipid meal, every scribble on a clipboard, every blip on the heart machine was a reminder of my failure. I silenced the damning voices in my head with various pills. I thought I would never be able to pay off my many student loans until I eventually found a job that could hoist me out of my debt and beyond. Now I help bring little babies into the world and am sure I'm much better off than someone who has to deal with the gores of surgery. Plus it doesn't hurt to be able to afford new pair of shoes every now and then.

I've delivered over five hundred babies. I keep a record of each and every one in my little pink book that I carry in my purse. It's for my eyes only. Sometimes, at night, I lie in bed and wonder how all those sweet little babies are doing. Of course all babies are special, but some are more special than others. Some babies you just never forget.

June screams until she can't hold the note anymore. It ends in a blunt groan.

"We're almost there," I assure her, snapping off my glove and being careful to not touch anything with my bare hands. I never touch anything in a birthing room without gloves on.

She has dilated to eight centimetres. It's almost time to push.

She claws my arm. I wince.

"I can't do it," she says, "I can't do it."

Her grey lips plead with me.

"Of course you can," I say, reclaiming my wrist.

She begins to cry. Small, sad sobs.

"You're going to be just fine. It will be like we practised, remember?"

Sob.

I've always been fascinated with babies. The way they grow in their mother's wombs, taking the lion's share of blood nutrients. How they enter the world, blue and kicking, probably wishing they could go back to their dark, sticky cocoon. Their clenched little fists, their eyes like schoolyard marbles. Even after five hundred and twenty eight babies I still wonder at these sublime little creatures.

I can see that June is exhausted. Her hospital gown is soaked with perspiration. I put a cold compress on her forehead and offer her a sip of water but she won't have it. She is ivory pale. I check her vitals. Her heartbeat is regular but her blood pressure is high. She's not bleeding so there doesn't seem to be anything to worry about.

Tuesdays are always a midwife's busiest day. More babies are born on a Tuesday the world over than any other day of the week. Sundays are, typically, the slowest. Late summer is the busiest time of the year. Boy babies outnumber girl babies, but they also have a lower survival rate. Jacob is the most popular name for boy babies, and Emily for girls.

June seems to have come round and is breathing well. She's getting ready for the next contraction. They are less than a minute apart now. She begins to growl. It looks like we are in business. I beep the nurse that will look after June while I'm busy with the baby. I listen to the baby's heartbeat and it is beautifully even.

Nurse Spencer arrives with a polystyrene cup of tea.

"I thought you could do with it," she froths. "It's Susan, isn't it?"

I look at her blankly. The unruly curls pinned down with her white cap, the straining uniform, the equine teeth.

"Your name?" she prods.

"Oh. Yes. It's Susan."

"It wasn't a trick question."

I half-laugh.

"I'm sorry, it's been a long labour."

I don't want to take the cup but I do.

"It'll be over soon."

I can see that she's not sure of me. She likes people who smile constantly. The tea is cool and weak. She probably doesn't like working with new people.

I'm temping at the moment. Usually I freelance. Homebirths are my speciality. I move around a lot. I like change. I never drive the same car for more than a few months. I'm always colouring, cutting, or extending my hair. I buy new clothes in each new town. It's a kind of tradition, now. I give the 'old' ones away, usually to the Salvation Army. I like to travel light.

June has given up screaming and has settled instead for a primal groan. Nurse Spencer is talking to her in a low, comforting voice. I crunch the polystyrene cup into a ball and slip it into my pocket. I snap on a new pair of latex gloves. My fingers slide into June easily and I can feel that her cervix is now open a full ten centimetres. If all goes well we'll have a baby within the next few minutes.

"Are you ready to push?" I ask her.

I first met June three months ago when she was interviewing midwives. She's the reason I came to Saint Mary's Hospital. I drove the three hundred kilometres to the interview and never went back home. June wanted me and it's a nice town so there was no reason for me to go anywhere else. Sister Angelika looked me up and down and through pursed lips agreed that the hospital would take me on a temporary basis. My new look had worked. Shiny, nut-coloured hair and matching brown contact lenses, all bought from the pharmacy on the way over. A woolly cardigan to go over my collared dress, showing only just enough neck to reveal the third pharmacy purchase: a cheap gold cross necklace.

"Push!" nurse Spencer urges.

June's screwed-up face is flushed now. Her clamped teeth escape her grimace.

"That's good, June. You're doing well."

Pushing, groaning, breathing.

"A few more pushes and we'll have a beautiful little boy."

A frustrated sob. A half-scream.

"We're almost there. I can see his head!"

Nurse Spencer tap dances.

With a bellow from June her baby's head crowns. Before asking her to push again I check that the umbilical cord is not wrapped around his neck.

"The hardest part is over, June," I say, "all you have to do is finish off now."

She half-nods at me. The rest of the baby slips smoothly out.

"He's out," I say, and the nurse dances again.

He's not breathing. His skin is blue. I clap him on

the bum and we all hold our breath until his small cry peals out.

Nurse Spencer checks up on June while I attend to the baby. I clamp and sever the umbilical cord in a practised motion. I carry him to the corner of the room, put the suction tube into his mouth and gently wipe his skin. I weigh him. Then I swaddle him tightly in a soft cream cotton receiving blanket.

"You did such a good job," Nurse Spencer is telling June.

"Is he okay?" pants June.

"He's perfect! He'll be with you in a minute. He's just having his toes counted."

June closes her eyes and surrenders to the snowflake-patterned white sheets of her bed. Nurse Spencer fusses around her.

"Nurse," I say calmly, "call the doctor."

Her face jumps.

"Is there something the matter?" she whispers.

The words, now so familiar, need no thought.

"Just call the doctor."

She paces out of the room.

I take the syringe of tranquiliser out of my hand-bag, attach the needle, and puncture June's IV tube with it. I have learnt to not leave marks. As I empty the syringe, her eyes flutter open and then close again. I pick up the baby, plug his searching mouth with a pacifier, and ease him into the padded tote bag I had hidden behind the metal cabinet. I zip it up. The material is light and breathable but keeps the baby warm. This has almost become too easy. My soles squeak on the polished linoleum floor as I leave the room and turn the corner. I smile sweetly as I pass Sister Angelika in the corridor.

Within two minutes of dispatching the nurse I walk out of the hospital, gently swinging my bag. The sun is bright, the trees are green, and I have a new town to get to.

10

OFF THE HINGE

The woman at the counter is looking at me very strangely, as if I am a giant, or a midget, or as if I am wearing a shiny salmon for a hat.

'Am I wearing a shiny salmon?' I ask her. Shiny spotty silver singing salmon. Karaoke Sashimi. She blinks her marbles at me. Confusion darkens her face. I don't want to upset her.

'I don't want to upset you,' I say. 'All I need is some milk, for my tea.'

'Milk?' she says, happy that now she knows what I need and can help me.

'Milk for my tea,' I say, and she smiles. I smile back. I am happy. This is good. 'And some bone buttons, and a mouse.'

Her happy teeth disappear again, like shy sea pebbles in the tide.

'Sea pebbles,' I say.

'What?' she says. 'A mouse?'

'A mouse!' I say, laughing in her face. Funny! A mouse.

She moves away from me. Maybe she thinks I am a mouse. Maybe she is afraid of mice. If I am a mouse or not, I mean no harm. I take out my wallet. I need to pay for the milk. I search the empty counter for the white bottle.

'Where is the milk?' I ask.

'We don't sell milk here,' the lady says.

'You don't sell MILK?' I am astonished. Aghast. What kind of shop doesn't sell milk? How will I make my tea?

'I think you might be in the wrong place,' she says,

windmilling her arms at her wares. 'You see, this is an antique shop.'

I look around. I see ceramic soup tureens and copper candlesticks and crystal snifters. I want to smash the crystal, although I can't think why. I'm not angry. Maybe I just want to see what will happen. I want to see the rainbow shards and splinters. I want to feel powerful. I want to destroy these pretty things and stomp them into the floor and lift my arms and bellow like King Kong.

'Is there someone I can call for you?' asks the crystal snifter lady. She is worried. I know this because her voice is a tall, pink, wobbling jelly. Raspberry?

'Hmm?'

'Your husband?' she says, then, looking at my naked ring finger: wrinkled. 'Or a ... friend?'

I don't know why she has to mention Larry. What does Larry have to do with antiques? I spin the imaginary wedding band. It's something I used to do.

'I can call someone for you, and make you a cup of tea, while you wait.'

'I *would* like a cup of tea,' I say. The truth is I feel like I could kill a cup of tea. No, that's not right. How does the saying go?

'Let me pay you for it,' I say, paging through my wallet. How much does a cup of tea cost? I have no idea.

50 cents? 50 rand? Maybe it costs 50 cents but they will charge me 50 rand and then they would have 49 rand 50 of mine that they don't deserve. That they've fleeced me of. It appears that antique dealers are not to be trusted.

'No, no,' she says, hiding her marbles with eyelid-skin at seeing my open wallet. 'It's not necessary. Really. Please, take a seat.'

She motions towards an over-waxed mahogany piece carved with balls and claws. It has a balding maroon velvet seat. There is dust in the air. I can't see it but it is tickling the end of my nose.

I don't want to sit on the antique chair. It looks un-trustworthy. Also, it might bite me. I put my hands behind my back to protect my buttocks. Ball and claws. Buttock. Buttock. Buttock.

'Buttock,' I say, but the lady has vanished. She has time-travelled to the next century where she is looking for a kettle to boil. I am glad. Now I don't have to sit on the buttock-biting chair. I think she will probably be a long time, so I will leave this old copper candlestick shop and go to get the milk.

On the way out I pick up a plate. The heirloom is seashell-thin: begging to be broken. Someone has drawn a French pastoral scene on it, in powder blue. It begins to burn in my hands. I am torn between taking it with me, and throwing it against the floor as hard as I can. I want to take it in my bag. I want it to shatter. I want to hold it against my chest like a newborn baby. I want it in smithereens. The word 'smithereens' makes me think of polystyrene.

'Polystyrene,' I say. I slip the plate into my bag and step out of the shop.

There are lots of people on this road. Lots of cars. I need to walk upright so that the shiny salmon doesn't fall off my head. In school they would award certificates for deportment. Walk like you have a rodding iron for a backbone and get a gilt-edged certificate. A golden backbone. A Mary Poppins song pops into my head. The one about flying kites. There it is, the song, barbed in my brain, and the words come over and over. LET'S go FLY A KITE, UP to the HIGHEST HEIGHT. The lyrics boomerang between my temples. I hum along. I try not to stomp in rhythm with the song. I don't want people to stare. Like that man over there in the silly chef's pants, with his arms crossed in front of his chest, white smoke trailing out of his nose like a magic dragon. As if he has swallowed fire.

He is looking at me. How rude. I will just walk right past and ignore him. He keeps looking. His eyebrows are steep, and too dark. Much too dark. I don't like them one bit.

'Buttock,' I say, and keep walking.

The sun is a big hot ball travelling the sky in slow-motion. I'm really thirsty now. I find a shop that looks like it might sell milk. I go straight up to the counter. Spit-Spot. No dawdling.

'Do you sell milk?' I ask, perhaps a trifle loudly. A

trifle loudly. A loud trifle. Goodness. That sounds delicious. I would like to eat a Loud Trifle. It sounds like something out of an Enid Blyton fantasy novel.

The young man in the shop is too skinny. He could do with eating a Loud Trifle. I want to tell him so, but what good will come of that? I bite my tongue.

'Milk? Like, a glass of milk?' he says, as if he doesn't understand. As if milk is a philosophical concept that is difficult to grasp. His hair is pointing in all different directions as if he has just woken up from a particularly frightening dream. His skin has writing on it. He could do with a good wash.

'A bottle of milk, for my tea,' I say.

'So you want *tea?*'

Perhaps he needs more than a good wash. A lesson in English comprehension, for one.

'Yes,' I say slowly. 'Milk. For. Tea.'

He is embarrassed now (I would be too!) and rubs his head pelt possum pear.

'So,' he says, cleaning the sleep from his eye, 'do you want tea, or do you want milk?'

Am I not speaking clearly? Is the idea of buying milk just too complicated for mere mortals like this dirty skeleton to comprehend? I feel instantly exhausted by the dire hopelessness of the human race. I feel drained. Doomed. I need to sit down. Luckily there are lots of tables and chairs in this shop. Perhaps it is a furniture shop. The chairs here are not dusty and they are not buttock-biters. It feels good to rest my golden spine. The grubby skeleton brings me a glass of milk and a cup of tea. This does not help my cause whatsoever. I need to leave, to find a bottle of milk to take home with me. Poor Larry, he has probably keeled over from his lack of tea this morning. Keel peel kipper. Shiny Salmon. I can't drink the tea on the table in front of me, as much as I want to. It wouldn't be fair to Larry. How would he feel, if he saw me here, knocking back a good, hot cuppa while he is in the very process of keeling over from the thirst? No. I can't take a sip. Not one. I need to leave. I make it out the door and 3 shops down before the un-washed calls me.

'Your milk!' he shouts. 'Your tea!'

I scrabble over the cobblestones. I can smell the sea in the air. I'm afraid the skelly will follow me but he just stands there, wiping his hands on his floury apron of defeat. I don't know what I was doing, looking to buy milk at a furniture shop. My head needs checking. I try to swallow the dryness in my throat.

I want to walk faster now, but am feeling light-headed. When last did I eat? I keep going. There must be some kind of corner shop, some kind of convenience store. Damn it, what kind of street is this, anyway? I shiver; my golden backbone is chilled from head to tail. Perhaps my pelvis is turning into metal, too. What kind of award would present you with a golden pelvis? I'm not sure I'd like to know. I should have had that tea at that furniture shop. It looked like a good cup of tea. It's not easy to find a good cup of tea. Larry wouldn't have been happy, but then, is Larry ever happy?

The light is evaporating. The sun has had enough of shining. I feel a bluebottle of adrenaline shoot through my veins. How can it be so late? Larry will be worried! He'll be furious. I'm quite sure that I left the house this morning, not more than an hour ago! What has happened to the day? I wrap my cardigan around me. I can't go home without milk, though. Then it'll become A Story. No, no, no. I will not go home empty-handed. I will not be butt of yet another bitter joke. I'll try one more shop. I could assassinate a cup of tea. No. I could … execute a cup of tea?

The wind is picking up and I feel the grey shadows creeping along the pavements and up my legs. I count the signs shouting 'CLOSED' until I run out of fingers but then there is one store with a front door flung open with golden light and laughter. I dispense with formalities and just yell 'Milk!' to the people inside. They are wearing cocktail dresses and sipping rubies from glasses. When they notice me they stop and peer over. There are too many steep eyebrows on this street. I don't like it one bit.

'Milk!' I yell again. I lift my wallet at them, as if to signal that I will pay for it. I don't care how much it costs. I will pay 50 rand for a bottle of milk if that's what they want. I hear dead leaves gusting along the street. They flutter up against the glass façade.

There are tears in my eyes, but I'm not sure why. I blink them away and see art on the walls. I want to tell them about the antique lady who is now in another time-dimension searching for teabags and sugar, and the barely-skinned skeleton with writing on him. I want to tell them about Larry who will most definitely have something to say about me going out for a bottle of milk for tea and disappearing for 10 hours.

I'll never hear the end of it.

My mouth is dry; glued together. I try to use spit to un-stick my tongue.

I'm about to tell them that I have an extremely fragile plate in my bag when I see the distaste in their painted faces. They don't want me here. They don't want to hear about my bottle of milk. There may be luxurious light all around them but there is no light in their eyes. They are all wearing masks. They are aliens. Not the kind that abduct you.

I turn around too quickly and stumble; hurting my bad ankle. I feel the twinge all the way up the left side of my body. I grit dry teeth in lieu of a gasp. I limp.

'Wait!' I hear from behind me, but I don't stop, because I don't want to talk to the aliens, even if they don't want to abduct me.

'Wait!' I hear again, closer, almost in my ear. There is a young woman at my elbow. I recoil at her extra-terrestrial touch. She is breathing hard, as aliens are known to do. It's the atmosphere here on earth; the thin air. It's not good for them.

'I must get on,' I say. The sooner I leave this alien art gallery the better.

'Where do you stay?' she asks. 'Let me call you a taxi. My treat.'

That's what aliens say just before they abduct you.

'No, no, no,' I say, trying to get away. She laserbeams my face with hers until she no longer looks like an alien wearing a mask but a real person with tiny red veins in her eyes and pores on her nose. Lunar craters. I stare at her nasal moonscape. I don't know how she did that. It's a good trick.

'That's a good trick,' I say to her.

'Please,' she says. 'It's cold outside and you're hardly wearing anything.'

This takes me by surprise. I look down and see that I am still in my nightgown. A pair of dog-gummed slippers and a moth-eaten cardigan complete the look souk sunny. Funny.

Bone buttons.

'I can't go home without the milk,' I say.

'I don't have any,' she says, looking around at the rubies and champagne. 'If I did, I would give it to you.'

I don't want her alien milk, anyway. It would probably taste like mice. Larry wouldn't approve. I reclaim my elbow and leave.

The street is dark. The shops are closed. I don't know how I'm going to find milk now. The people have all packed up and gone home. They don't see me skipping over cracks in the pavement in my white cotton dress. They don't see an ancient white fairy gliding down their lonely black road.

I am so thirsty, I feel like I could drink the moonlight. It would taste like home-made ginger-beer. It would prickle and pop in the back of my throat.

'Stop,' says the tall man with the massive dog's head on his shoulders. I have never seen such a big dog's head. I have never seen a man with a dog's head. He is a Husky. He has those keen blue Husky eyes and black triangles for ears which would disappear against the night if he wasn't in the habit of shaking them at me. There is something in his voice that makes me obey. No, that's not right. It's not something *in* his voice but his *actual* voice that makes me stop. A Husky's voice will do that.

The wind is a wet sheet on my back, but I don't move. Perhaps he is the antique watchdog, sent from an outer-century.

'You've come for the plate?' I ask. 'I didn't mean to take it.'

'No,' says the dogman, with the ginger-beer reflection in his eyes.

'The plate is of no use where we are going,' he says. He adjusts his handsome black cloak. It looks warm.

'We?' I say, shivering.

'We,' he says.

'How can a plate be of no use? A plate is always of use,' I say. I don't mean to argue with the Husky but, ultimately, common sense must prevail.

'That is true,' he pants, 'but broken plates are less useful.'

I stick my hand into my bag and feel the daggers of the broken plate. Smithereens. Polystyrene. I am sorry. When the crystal-snifter lady gets back from her time-travelling I will apologise, and pay for the plate. I look down at my wallet, wondering if I have enough money.

'What are you doing?' asks the Husky.

'I'm counting my money,' I say. 'This is my wallet.'

'That's a funny-looking wallet,' he says. I want to say that he is a funny looking man, or a funny looking dog, but I don't. I don't want to be rude. I look down at my wallet again and see what he means. It's not a wallet at all, but a book. No wonder no-one would sell me a bottle of milk. I

was trying to pay them with a secondhand paperback.

'What is the story about?' says the dog. He speaks
right into my face, like dogs do, but he does not
have dog-biscuit breath. Perhaps he doesn't eat dog
biscuits. His whiskers are fishing lines that cast
around for things. I don't know what things yet.

I look down again, turn the book over in my hands.
It is familiar to the touch. I have held this book for
a long time. The cover art is blurry. I can't read the
title. I try to concentrate, to force it into focus. Finally, the words appear. OFF THE HINGE, it says.
It rings a bell.

The dogman tries again: 'Do you know what it's
about?'

'What are all stories about?' I say.

'Love,' pants the canine. 'Loneliness. Redemption.'

'Yes,' I say. I watch his pink tongue vibrate. 'Where
are we going?'

He starts to howl. You'd think that it would make me

feel uncomfortable, standing there on the street, watching a wolfman howl, but I'm not. It feels right. I won't join in, even though I am tempted to. It's a beautiful sound. When he stops howling it's like a sound-vacuum. Like the world will never be complete again until the howling recommences. I'm amazed at how I have spent my whole life without it.

'Is it time to go?' I ask.

'Yes,' says the dog. 'Are you ready?'

'I don't know.'

All of a sudden it's like being in a stress-dream where I am woefully unprepared: sitting naked in class during an exam, or realising the morning of my wedding day that I had forgotten to buy a white dress. My underarms start to perspire, although I can't see how. I thought there was no moisture left in my body.

'What about my husband?' I say. 'He'll keel over without me.'

'Larry?' says the dog.

'Of course, Larry,' I say. 'Do I have any other husbands?'

'Larry left a long time ago,' says the wolfman. 'You do not need to worry about him.'

There's a lightning bolt of recognition in my brain. The keeling over of Larry is not a thought, but a memory.

'He left?'

'Metaphysically speaking,' barks the dog.

'He died?' I say, and as the words leave my mouth I know that it is true.

'There is no such thing as 'death',' says the giant dog head.

I am relieved. Mostly because I am no longer in trouble with Larry.

'What do I need to take with me?' I say. 'I suppose a shiny salmon will not come in handy?'

'I have eaten the salmon,' says the dogman. 'It has served its purpose.'

I feel for my hat and it is true: there is nothing on

top of my head.

'To be prepared,' says the Husky, 'you will need a book, a baby, and a bag.'

Oh dear, I think. Where will I find a baby at this late hour?

'Look inside your bag,' pants the dog. I peer inside, expecting to see the French shards, but instead there is a tiny mewling baby with writing on her skin. It is the powder-blue pastoral scene. I lift the baby out and hold her to my chest. I shush her and tell her that everything will be alright. I pat her back until she's quiet.

'Will there be milk, where we are going?' I ask, not without hope. He fixes his ginger-beer cataracts on me.

'There will be milk.'

I'm not convinced. He makes it sound so easy to find milk, and I know that it's not. My mouth is a cotton ball.

Buttock.

'Will there be enough?' I ask. The tattooed baby sleeps peacefully in my arms.

'Where we are going,' he barks, 'there is enough of everything. Come gently, now. It is time.'

'But, specifically, milk?'

'There will be rivers of milk,' he fibs. A dairy-white lie. 'Cream waterfalls. Gushing dams of liquid lactose. A deluge of moo-juice. Enough to bath in. To swim in. To canoe in. To sink an ocean-liner in.'

The Husky takes my face in his hands. They are velvet. He opens his mouth and leans towards me with his non-biscuity breath. I think he's going to kiss me but then his shiny salmon tongue is combing my hair. He tames my grey bird's nest. He grooms me as if I am a stray kitten. Perhaps that is what I am.

My eyes are watering again. I think it must be the relief. He swishes his coat until it covers all three of us and we begin to walk together. His whiskers trawl the night air. We walk off the edge of the Earth, where the universes are hinged together. The night explodes with stars.

The metallic tasting meteor-light cuts through my every need.

It's a different kind of milk, thinks the Husky, and I can hear his thoughts.

Of course, I think back at him. I get it. When you have this, you don't need milk. It's the same as having enough milk to canoe in. It's actually better.

Yes, pants the Husky. You get it. It's better.

11

STICKY FINGERS

I learnt how to keep a secret when I was three years old.

It started on an ordinary day — a sunny Jo'burg afternoon. I was in my mom's arms while she was buying cigarettes from the sweet counter at Checkers. She used to smoke the Dunhill 30s that came in a wide red and gold box, (with gold foil inside!), and a white underside that was perfect for scribbling shopping lists and working out math problems. When making this smoker's stop after doing the grocery shopping, she'd always let us choose a few little chocolates for the sweetie bowl at home. Maybe it made her feel less guilty about spending money on cigarettes, or smoking around us. Maybe it was just her being kind; even on a teacher's salary she was always generous.

She'd give us each a silver bowl and my older brother and I would be allowed to choose a few different treats. We always went for the chocolates – the other stuff was a waste of time. My favourites were the chocolate-peanut clusters, followed closely by the chocolate-coconut clusters. The bowls were then weighed and paid for: a sweet ritual.

That day, while everyone else's eyes were on the scale, including mine, a little three-year-old hand reached out towards the sweets and, before I knew it, there was a chocolate toffee finger melting in my pocket.

I don't know what made me steal it. Mom had already bought me the chocolates I had wanted (I'm not even sure I liked chocolate toffee fingers). Perhaps I was just born an opportunist. Maybe my kleptomania was inherent to my make-up, along with my bad temper, green eyes and big feet.

Sometimes I wonder if I would still be a thief if that first incident hadn't happened … if I hadn't experienced that hot thrill of having something that didn't belong to me.

If, for some reason, I had resisted that first childish impulse to grab, perhaps my restless heart wouldn't be forever waiting for The Next Nice Thing To Steal.

Was I too young to understand right from wrong? Perhaps. I did show off my loot the moment we got into the car, which makes me think that I didn't know what I had done was wrong. Wasn't it quite clever of me to get something for nothing? I don't remember if I was expecting praise or punishment. I did learn then that I shouldn't show anyone what I had stolen, no matter how urgent the desire becomes. That's when I learnt how to keep a secret.

When I was five I kidnapped two dolls from nursery school. I sneaked them out in my scruffy cardboard suitcase. It wasn't so much 'stealing' in my mind, then, it was more the fact that I loved the dolls so much that I thought they should be living at home with me. Their names were Nadia and Devon. Once the stowaways were discovered, my mother marched me to the teacher to return them, and apologise. The teacher was so very kind about it – not only did she not scold me, but she agreed that, as I was such a good 'mother' to the dolls, I should be allowed to keep them. She was sure that they would be happier with me. Looking back now, I wonder if this confused my developing moral compass.

Whatever caused it, bad genes or bad luck, I am, and (most likely always will be), a thief. It took me a while to admit it, but that doesn't make it any less true. There is no arguing with the two hundred and sixty four lipsticks I have stashed under my bathroom sink, or the army of restaurant salt and pepper cellars that take up an entire double-cupboard in the kitchen. In my 20s I referred to myself as a 'collector'. I was making a stand against soulless industrialisation and crass materialism: 'Look,' I thought, 'I can take this without anyone even *noticing.*'

Row upon row of similar trinkets: my cupboards looked like Andy Warhol installations. I thought I was smart, ironic. I wasn't fooling anyone.

Sometimes I take things for specific reasons. I was at a cocktail party a few months ago and the hostess was this awful person. She had a horsey face and kept guffawing all over the place. She kept forgetting my name and calling me 'love', and I know it was because I'm a housewife and she thinks I don't matter. I turned my back on her soggy canapés but it wasn't enough: I knew I'd have to take something of hers, and I did. She didn't deserve to have the sweet ceramic rabbit miniature I found in her display cabinet, and I was certain he was much happier when he left in my clutch later that night.

It could also be due to nominative determinism. You know, like when your name is Bolt and you become the fastest sprinter in the world. Or Candy, and you become a stripper. Maybe that last example isn't such a good one; that's more like just changing your name to suit your talent. My name is Nicolette, and people call me Nicky or Nick. It's quite funny, I think, and I catch myself wanting to tell people, but of course, I can't.

It's lonely, being a klepto. So much of your existence revolves around your conquests and close calls, but you can never share that part of your life with other people. Last week I took the most beautiful orange and cream silk scarf from Poetry (scarves are one of the easiest things to steal, apart from panties and lipstick) – but I can't tell anyone about it. It has the most charming elephant print on it. I can't even wear it, because if Derek, my husband, sees it, he'll demand to see the receipt.

Sometimes I fantasize about an online dating site that caters to people like me. Of course I wouldn't actually date anyone – I'm happily married! – but it would be wonderful to just meet some like-minded people and share our stories.

Derek keeps giving me more cash. He sneaks it into my wallet and I pretend that I don't notice. I already have two credit cards that he pays off every month. He has always had so much money … it frustrates him to not be able to pay to make this problem go away. But it's not about money. He doesn't understand.

My best friend, Sylvia, is the only one I can really talk to, but I can't tell her everything either. She is one of the least judgmental people I know, but even she has her limits. I have to be careful to select only the stories I am bursting to tell, and hide everything else, like the fake pearls I took from my sister-in-law's jewellery box on Saturday, and the sandalwood-scented candle I got from the esoteric shop at Rosebank Mall. Esoteric shops are so easy to lift from: they are all too often dimly lit, have poor security measures, and the shop assistants simply don't expect their customers to steal. Bad karma, and all of that.

When I hold back from telling Sylvia for a few weeks she gets this bright look in her eyes. 'You're getting better!' she'll say. Or, 'You've turned a corner!'

She can be so naïve.

She's never really had any money, not much anyway, but I'm sure she hasn't stolen a thing in her life. A few years ago she made me start writing down, item for item, the things I was taking. She thought I was in denial about the extent of my 'problem' (I'm not). But I enjoyed the exercise of recording my acquisitions, and I still do it. I have 12 (stolen) notebooks full of excited entries. They read like accountant's ledgers. The pages are well thumbed ... one of my favourite things to do is to go through the lists and remember the moments they brought with them. It makes me feel like a 'collector' again. It makes it more real, in a way. More ... honest. The books are stacked underneath our bed. Only Sylvia knows about them.

I met Sylvia years ago at one of Derek's company's functions. They worked in the same building but had never met. I actually introduced them, and now we're all great friends. We've got a lot in common. Over the years she's become part of the family. The kids love her. Did I mention we have kids? A four- and a six-year-old – a boy and a girl (I resisted the urge to name them Nadia and Devon). I'm sure that we look like the picture-perfect family to some. To those who don't know about my habit. Sylvia is like the kids' fairy godmother, always wooing them with gifts and food.

She's like my fairy godmother too, I guess. A couple of years ago I was caught shoplifting a pair of Dolce & Gabana sunglasses from Sandton City.

Depending on your technique, sunglasses can be an easy lift, because you end up trying so many pairs on, there are bound to be some floating around the shop, unattended to. You have to do it when the shop is relatively busy — sales are always a good time — and you should arrive with a similar pair to the ones you want to nick, preferably perched on your head. Once you choose a pair, you replace the old ones with the new, *et voila,* out you flounce with a new pair of shades.

This has worked for me over and over, but on that unlucky day the security guard was paying attention. Perhaps my lipstick was too red: it was Revlon New Cherry. Bold make-up on a shoplifting spree is never a good idea; people don't trust women whose lipstick is too bright. But one gets complacent and neglects the rules. I hadn't been caught for so long that I stopped believing it could happen. Started thinking I had some kind of magical power. Ignored the bad karma of stolen lipstick.

So I made the switch quite near to the exit, and then turned to walk out, and next thing there was a strong hand grabbing me, like a headmaster would

yank the arm of a troublesome child. It was shock-
ing, but expected, at the same time. I tried to act
confused, concerned, then indignant, but I could
see the guard wasn't buying it. He was quiet and
kept glancing up at the red LED light of the security camera, as if waiting for someone to come
down and give him the go-ahead to slap some cuffs
on me. After a perfunctory exchange on his walkie-
talkie, he escorted me through the mall and sat me
down in a dingy office near the food court. There
was another stern-looking man there. All I could
smell was Cinnabon.

They weren't sure if they were going to press
charges, and wanted to speak to my husband before 'taking any steps'. I gave them Sylvia's number
instead. An hour later she had charmed and cajoled
the two men into giving me a warning (well, a
warning and a life-time ban from entering the
store). She made up this story about how my husband was having an affair and I was having a minor
nervous breakdown. I was impressed at what a
convincing liar she was — I had never guessed it.
From then on she called me 'Sticky Fingers'. She'd

poke me in the ribs and say 'Take that, Sticky Fingers.'

The smell of cinnamon still unsettles me.

The next time I was caught I wasn't that lucky. Sometimes I wonder if I actually *wanted* to get caught. Either way, I guess that it would have happened sooner or later. I mean, I wasn't going to stop stealing, so it was inevitable. My lucky streak, my magical power, wasn't going to last forever. I had had so many close calls over the years, over a lifetime: my Sticky Finger Magic was due to run out.

Derek and I were staying in a luxury hotel in Camps Bay, with a room that overlooked the sea. The kids were with his mother for the weekend, and we decided at the last minute to hop on a plane to Cape Town. We were pretending to be spontaneous: it's something rich married people do to try to keep the relationship exciting. It's weird, because it's like you're pretending to be someone else for the weekend: someone young, childless, passionate, romantic. And you try to reconnect with your significant other, but he is also pretending to be that other, lighter, person, but really neither of you are yourselves. So you drink more than usual and have kinkier sex than usual, but when Monday rolls around and he is pulling out his hair looking for his favourite tie for a meeting and you are wiping toothpaste off your toddler's cheeks and this is your real life and did the weekend in Cape Town actually even happen?

But there we were, in the hotel spa, after a full body Swedish massage and a quickie in the Rasul chamber. We went to our respective change-rooms to shower and before I left I did what I always do — I checked all the lockers. It's like checking a casino slot machine or a basement parking ticket machine for abandoned coins, except that some women are lulled into such a secure stupor by their privileged lifestyles that they don't even bother to lock away their things. I got three quarters of the way through when I hit the jackpot: a shiny new snakeskin Louis Vuitton handbag, with matching wallet and belt. The bag was too big to steal, and I had no need for the belt, so I took the wallet. It was a thing of beauty, not more than a few days old. The fact that it was a wallet meant that they would probably assume that a member of staff took it, for the cash, although I left behind her jewellery. It was gaudy: diamonds and Tanzanite. I held the necklace against my collarbone to see how it would look, just as a matter of interest. It confirmed what I already knew: blue stones are not my style.

A lady in a white spa bathrobe came in just as I was sliding the wallet into my own handbag. I played it cool, pretended that I was doing nothing unusual. I was just a woman putting her wallet into her bag. But, unfortunately for me, the robed lady happened to be the owner of the Louis Vuitton. It took a while for her to register what I was doing. I think she must have first thought: Oh, look, that lady has the same wallet as me. But then her eyes travelled to her locker, saw the door was open, saw that it had been plundered. Her face, previously scrubbed and blissful-looking, jumped into ferocious mode, and she proceeded to throw the biggest hissy fit I have seen. She was like a toddler on a double espresso. The words she was shouting at me didn't even make sense. I tried to calm her down, explain that it was a misunderstanding. I thought that it was my bag but then I realised I had brought my *other* bag, so I was putting it back. It's when I saw the jewellery that I had realised that it wasn't my locker. Tanzanite, I said, I never wear Tanzanite. That's what made me realise.

It was an unlikely story, but weaker ones had worked before. People are desperate to believe the best in other people.

… But not this manic madwoman. She seemed half outraged, half delighted to have a bit of drama in her day. Despite my constant assurances that she had misinterpreted the situation, she turned and fled the room to call security. I used my towel, still damp from the shower, to quickly wipe down her locker and the things of hers I had touched. Now it was her word against mine.

I glided out and headed in the opposite direction to the noise she was creating at the spa reception. I left through the back door and scuttled my way up to our hotel room. Derek was asleep, naked, on the bed, and I sat on our patio, looking at the sea, waiting for the knock at the door.

It took the hotel manager 20 minutes to figure out my name and room number. It had been staring out at him from the spa appointment book. He knocked softly at first — it was easy to ignore — then louder, and he started calling my name. Derek stumbled out of bed, confused but overly alert, the way you are when your nap is (rudely) interrupted. I threw a gown at him before I opened the door.

The man doing the knocking looked apologetic the moment he saw us.

'Terribly sorry!' he kept saying. 'Terribly sorry to inconvenience you, but could you come down to the hotel reception?'

'What is this about?' Derek demanded.

'Terribly sorry! There seems to be some kind of … I'm sure it's a misunderstanding.'

'Is there a problem?' my husband asked, still pale from sleep.

'There may not be?' said the manager. They looked at each other for a good time, perplexed.

'I know what this is about,' I said. 'Some crazy woman at the spa was accusing me of going through her locker. She was screaming at me ... she kicked up such a fuss!'

'Yes,' said the man, clearly relieved that he wouldn't have to make an allegation. Derek sighed.

'I should have complained,' I said to both of them. 'Being accosted like that.'

'Yes ...' said the man. 'A misunderstanding. That's what I told her. Will you come down so that we can clear it up?'

I paused. An innocent woman would have flown downstairs to clear her name. I sensed that if I went down there I would get into a vast amount of trouble. Both men sensed my hesitation. The manager's eyes pleaded with me to co-operate, to not make his day any more difficult than it already was. Derek jumped in.

'Well, was anything actually taken?' he asked.

'Taken?' said the man.

'Stolen! Was anything stolen from the woman?'

He paused. 'She's not making much sense — the lady — she's very upset. It's hard to know.'

'So can you please then explain to me why you don't just tell this lady to stop fabricating defamatory stories about my wife?'

I loved Derek so much in that moment. I felt so loved, so protected. He would get me out of this. He started to close the door, but the manager stopped him. Both men were gentle; there was no tussle. The man looked intensely uncomfortable. Eventually he blurted out: 'It's the ring!'

'What ring?' asked Derek.

'That ring,' he said, motioning to my left hand. I looked down and saw a diamond and Tanzanite ring on my index finger. I didn't even remember putting it on.

Things moved both quickly and agonisingly slowly from then. The police were called and I was arrested almost immediately, and charged, but the waiting in between was torture. Hours of staring at the grimy jail cell walls. Hours sitting on cheap cracked chairs waiting for some kind of admin to be done: paperwork to be processed, questions asked, answered and repeated *ad nauseum.* When they told me that my lawyer was getting on a plane to Cape Town I wanted to tell them — tell everyone — not to bother. I wanted to say, just give me the orange overalls and tin mug and bus me to wherever the hell I'm going to end up. At the time it seemed preferable to waiting for a lawyer to make his way to me all the way from Jo'burg.

Derek had, of course, hired the best lawyer money could buy, and when Mazarakis did finally walk into the beige room they were keeping me in I was very happy to see him. You would never have said that it was a Sunday, or that he had just been on a plane, with his sharp suit and alarmingly clear blue eyes. I, on the other hand, felt that I had aged 20 years in the last few hours. I looked different, felt different: I was a completely disparate person to the woman who had a loving husband and two beautiful children, or the woman who had had a massage overlooking the ocean that morning. My skin was whiter, thinner; my pores larger; my body vulnerable. The enchantment had been broken. I had been exposed for who I truly was.

Mazarakis was calm and measured, and explained what I was to expect in the next few hours, and days. I'd have to stay in custody overnight as they could only apply for bail on Monday morning. He was apologetic at that, as if it was his fault I had stolen the ring. He never asked me if I did actually steal anything — I think Derek must have told him about my 'problem'.

After bail was set, I was allowed to fly home with Derek. He was angry with me, cold, but still sat next to me on the plane despite lots of free seats in the first class cabin. It's a terrible feeling, knowing you have let someone down so badly. The exigent guilt settles into your body, your organs become heavy with dread.

We refused the complimentary Graham Beck brut, and the cheddar straws. They had no place in this new, upside-down world of ours. Derek had a Business Day open on his lap but I could tell he wasn't reading it. I could almost hear the thoughts crowding his head: 'What was she thinking?'; 'Why would she risk so much?'; 'What if she has to go to prison?'; 'She doesn't even *like* Tanzanite!' and, of course, 'What about the children? Who will be their mother?'

Of course, the same questions had been haunting

me for years, and I could never answer them. I am dishonest by nature, but this is true: if I could have fed my addiction in a less destructive way, I would have.

During the trial, Sylvia stayed at the house with the kids. She fed them, bathed them, took them to school. She kept photos of them in her wallet and on her phone to show me when we caught up, in snatched spells during proceedings. She brought paintings that they had done for me, showing us as the perfect little family, standing outside our perfect little house. I couldn't help noticing that the mother in the picture was starting to look more like Sylvia than me.

I was so grateful that she was there to support Derek; he was taking it very badly. She would sit next to him in court, with a brave face, positively glowing in comparison to him. Every time I caught his eye he gave me this pained expression, as if he already knew it was all over.

Sylvia brought me things from home — small comforts: pajamas, toiletries, books. Even homemade chocolate peanut butter cookies, that she had baked using my recipe, in my oven.

We would have won the case, Mazarakis said so. He said there was absolutely no evidence against me, apart from that damn ring, which he creatively — and successfully — explained away as a 'misunderstanding'.

There was no convincing evidence against me, until on the day of sentencing the prosecutor received a delivery from an anonymous source. It was a large brown box full of notebooks — my lifted ledgers — full of years of detailed entries of all the things I had stolen. Of course, they were in my handwriting, and covered with my fingerprints.

When I recognised the covers and realised what they were, it felt like I had been stabbed in the chest. A quick, nimble blade, between my ribs. In-and-out. And then a slow cold bleeding.

It turned out that I hadn't learnt how to keep a secret at all.

Only one person had known about those notebooks, and where they had been hidden. As the prosecutor introduced them to the court, and they were admitted as evidence, I looked at Sylvia, but she wouldn't return my gaze. It was then that I saw her hand on Derek's lap, and his hand on hers.

And I could hear her voice in my head, saying: 'Take that, Sticky Fingers'.

12

ESCAPE

'He's suicidal,' says The Father. The People laugh.

'Seriously,' he says, turning back to the braai and the hot spitting sausages.

The Mother clicks her tongue. Shakes her head. Tips warm Shiraz into her mouth.

'Don't be such a drama queen.'

I make my monkey noises and she hoists me, inelegantly, onto her lap. I warm my evening-chilled cheeks on her chest. The woman who sits in The Mother's usual chair shrieks with laughter.

'You're too much,' she warbles to The Father. 'You're just too much.' She wears her perfume in a cloud. The Mother shifts irritably on the couch. Perhaps it's not as comfortable as her usual chair.

'I'm being serious, Peg,' The Father says.

Peg? I think. That's a funny name for a big lady.

'Why do you say that?' the woman asks, once her belly has stopped jiggling. 'That the baby's suicidal?'

'He has absolutely no concept of danger,' says The Father.

'That's completely normal,' says The Mother. 'How is he supposed to know not to … not to crawl into a fire, for instance?'

'Surely they have some sense of self-preservation?' asks the man with the funny eyes who is eating all the potato chips.

'Ha!' shouts The Father, snapping his tongs. 'If only.'

I can smell red coals. Smoke and meat. Lamb chops.

'You can't expect him to know *not* to crawl into a fire,' says the Mother. 'He's a little baby. Look at the size of his head!'

'Hey?' says The Father.

'His brain is still tiny. His pre-frontal cortex hasn't been developed yet.'

'Pre-frontal cortexes have nothing to do with self-preservation. Besides, he has a bigger brain than Mojo and Mojo knows not to crawl into a fire.'

Mojo's ears shoot up at his name being mentioned. Do the humans need him? Is it time for a walk? A game? A snack? He gets up to investigate but then feels the nip in the air; decides to go back to sleep instead. He turns around and around on his bed before he feels he is in exactly the right position and then whimpers down.

'He's a dear little thing, isn't he?' says the Peg. She means Mojo, not me.

'Yes,' smiles The Mother. 'He's a darling pup. Lovely nature. Although he did chew up Dave's slippers the other day.'

'Ah, they were old,' says The Father. 'Good riddance.'

'And he ate one of Kade's toys. Naughty puppy,' says The Mother. She says 'naughty' but she's using her vanilla voice which means that she's not really cross.

'Kade didn't seem to mind.'

'As long as it wasn't his cuddle-bunny,' says The Mother.

I am holding Cuddle Bunny by his ear. That's my favourite way to hold him.

'Nice, for a lad to have a dog,' says the man with the funny eyes. 'I expect that they'll be good friends.'

'They are, already,' says The Father. 'Mojo is very good with him.'

With everyone's attention on the dog I leap off The Mother's lap and hurtle towards the verandah floor. I hit my head hard (but not hard enough). The People gasp. There is a shocked silence, and then I wail with all my might.

'My God,' says The Father, flinging the tongs down

and rushing towards me. He grabs me under the arms, lifts me up towards the light, inspects my forehead for injury. 'Did you just *drop* him?'

'No!' shouts The Mother, in pale skin. 'He just … he leapt off!'

My forehead throbs. It grows an egg. I wail and wail like an ambulance.

'You see?' he demands of the Peg and the man with funny eyes. 'You see what I mean?'

Peg clutches her pearls.

'I think you should stop drinking,' says The Father, eyeing out The Mother's wineglass.

'Don't blame me!' shouts The Mother. 'He jumped!'

I'm getting tired now. I tone my cries down to a sad blubbering. The Father hugs me and Bunny to his woolly chest.

'Is there any … damage?'

The man takes off his funny eyes, shines them on his flannel shirt, and puts them back on. He peers over at me as if I am a curiosity.

'Probably,' says The Father, roughly mussing my hair and kissing the top of my head.

'Mama,' I cry. 'Mama.'

'Poor little brain,' says The Mother, taking me gently and swaying me to the ballad in the background.

'Is there anything I can do?' asks the Peg. The man packs more chips into his mouth.

'Yes,' says The Mother. 'You can knit him some kind of cotton wool helmet. Some kind of … thud-guard. Or better yet, a full-body suit. A bubble-wrap onesie.'

'A what, dear?'

'She's joking,' says the chip man, dusting his greasy fingers.

'Kade would probably find a way to suffocate himself with the bubble-wrap,' sighs The Father.

I don't know why they call me 'Kade' when my name is Aaron. I wish I could tell them but the only words I have are 'Mama,' 'Up,' and 'Bye.' It's diffi-cult to describe my existential angst to them with such a limited vocabulary. How do I tell them that there's been a mistake? That I'm not supposed to be here, with them? That I don't belong in this body?

'It's very stressful,' says The Mother, pushing the coleslaw around on her plate.

'Of course it is!' says the Peg. 'Having small children is …'

'It's relentless,' says The Father. His hair has a new glint of grey.

'Exactly,' says The Mother. She holds a hand to her temple, as if she is the one with the egg.

I am patting Mojo. He is pretending to sleep. We are both good at that.

'I just never realised,' says The Mother, 'how … dangerous the world was, before I had Kade.'

'We spent a fortune baby-proofing this place before he was even born —'

'The pool net alone cost thousands —'

'But it's like he has a built-in danger-seeking radar.'

'If there is a sharp fork and a plug point he *will* find them both and force it in there,' says The Mother.

'If there's a ladder to climb —'

'— Or *anything* to climb —'

' — He'll climb as high as he can, and then fall.'

Or jump, I think.

'Or jump!' says The Father.

'He's like a little monkey, but without the balance,' says The Mother.

'A monkey with a death wish,' says The Father. He looks straight at me. There is affection in his frown.

The man with the funny eyes chuckles. He doesn't finish his boerewors roll. His stomach is full. He has eaten too many chips.

Chips! I think. I want some. I drop my bottle of milk and toddle over to the coffee table. I press my palm into the chip bowl. A chip sticks to my hand and I graze it off. So salty. I put all my fingers into my mouth. Yum.

'He's allowed chips?' asks the pearl-clutcher.

'Not really,' says The Father.

'Not at all,' says The Mother.

'I say,' says the man with the leftover roll on his plate, 'I say: let them shred twenty-rand notes if it keeps them quiet!'

The People laugh. I look up from my chip bowl and laugh, too. There are some spit-soggy chips in my open mouth. They look at me and laugh some more. The Mother moves towards me to take away the salty bowl. I protest.

'Shame, love,' says The Father. 'Just let him have them. It makes him happy.'

'They're not good for him,' says The Mother.

'You can't be afraid of everything, dear,' tuts the cloud of perfume.

'Easy for you to say,' mumbles The Mother under her breath.

'Here,' The Mother says to me, 'have some apple.'

She feels bad about taking the chips away. I grab

the peeled slice from her hand and jam it into my mouth. The cold fruit feels good on my gums. The sweet juice leaks. I grab another piece. I like holding food in both hands at once.

'Slowly!' she cautions. I inhale a big chunk. It's stuck. I can't breathe. The white flesh is like a cork in my throat.

Mojo is up like a shot, and barking madly.

'He's choking!' shouts The Father.

My eyes feel like they are going to pop.

Without hesitating, The Mother swoops, bending me over her haunches, so that I am upside-down with her knee buried in my stomach, and whacks me on the back so hard that I vomit all over the terracotta tiles. The apple cork is dislodged. There is a collective gasp. Air stings my lungs.

The Mother's cheeks are burning. Her eyes shine. Is she angry with me? She pins me to her breasts, not caring about the sour vomit gluing our chests together. Not angry. She starts shaking.

'Holy shit,' says The Father. 'Did that just happen?'

'I got such a fright,' cries The Mother into my scalp. 'I got such a fright.' Her limbs form a vice around me; I struggle, but she won't let me go. I relax. I burrow into her. I'm a grey mouse.

The apple-choke wasn't on purpose. It was just a happy accident. Sometimes that happens. Other times I have to get creative.

'Do you know,' says The Mother, once I am feigning sleep in the travel cot nearby and The People are discussing my imminent demise over Pavlova, 'that he climbed into the oven once?'

'No!' says the Peg, helping herself to more dessert, licking a crumb off her thumb. 'He didn't!'

'He did!' says The Mother, topping up her wine-glass. 'Don't look at me like that, David,' she snaps. 'I'm off duty now.'

The Mother calls The Father 'David' when she's upset.

'I wasn't looking at you!' says The Father. 'God knows after that we all need a stiff drink.'

The Mother blubs.

'Will you be alright, dear?' asks the Peg. 'You must have gotten such a shock.'

'He climbed into the OVEN,' she says. She wants to say more, but instead she zips her mouth closed and pushes her plate away.

'It happens. You said so, yourself. Babies don't know what is good for them,' says the man with cream on his moustache. He has found space for pudding even though he didn't finish his roll.

The Mother blubs some more. The Peg hands her a paper serviette off the table. She blows her nose. It's louder than I expected. Usually she only blows her nose loudly when we are alone.

'I'm not crying about the choking,' says The Mother. 'I'm crying because ...'

'Because you're exhausted!' says The Father. 'We don't blame you!'

'No,' says The Mother, dabbing at her nose and then making the serviette disappear in her fist. 'It's because he won't give up.'

'What do you mean?'

'If he's not flinging himself onto the floor or choking on an apple or climbing into the oven he'll do something else! It's like he won't stop until he … until he kills himself!'

'Karen!' they all say.

'That's not true.'

'You're just upset!'

'It's just been a bad day.'

'You said so yourself,' she yells at The Father. 'He's suicidal!'

The Father laughs. 'I was joking!' he says. 'Kind of.'

This is not good for anyone. I need to escape soon. I am fond of The Mother. I don't like to see her cry.

'Why don't we take him off your hands for a couple of hours, sometime?' suggests the man with the flannel shirt. 'How about next weekend? Saturday?'

The Peg looks at him strangely.

'What?' he says. 'We managed to keep our kids alive, didn't we?'

The Peg is clutching at her pearls again.

'You know, just so that you two can have a break. See a movie or something.'

The Mother guffaws. I think the wine is making her feel better.

'That's kind,' says The Father, 'Thank you.'

'I wouldn't be able to relax,' says The Mother. 'I feel like I am the only one who understands what a Kamikaze Kade is.'

It's *Aaron*, I think. I don't know what a Kamikaze is.

'I'm sure that within minutes he'd find a way to do some grievous bodily harm to himself.'

'Now who's being a drama queen?' asks The Father, touching her arm in a kind way.

'You know what happened at your mother's house,' she says, moving her arm away from his, knocking over her empty glass. It doesn't break. The man catches it before it rolls off the table, puts it out of the way.

'The one time I asked someone to look after him,' she says to The People, 'we almost lost him.'

'Lost him?' says the man.

'Literally and figuratively,' says The Father.

'What on earth …?' asks the Peg.

The Father clears his throat. 'He loves buttons, you see.'

'Buttons?'

'Pressing buttons,' says The Mother. 'All babies love pressing buttons.'

'So, my mom —' starts The Father, but The Mother jumps in.

'So Dave's mother leaves her house keys — with the garage door remote on them — lying around.'

'I'm sure she didn't just leave them *lying around*,' says The Father. 'I'm sure —'

'She did, David. Okay? She did. Because she wasn't bloody well thinking.'

'It's difficult to be cross with her, because she was doing us a favour by babysitting,' says The Father.

'Speak for yourself!' says The Mother.

'And the baby —?' says the Peg.

'Kade!' says the Mother.

'K— Kade opened the garage door?' asks saucer-eyed Peg.

The Father rubs his face with his hands; warms the back of his neck. Looks out into the dark leaves of the garden. The full moon floating in the pool.

'Not only did he open the door,' says The Mother, animated by the drink or her fury or both, 'but he CRAWLED OUT OF THE PROPERTY AND INTO THE STREET!'

'No!' says the Peg. 'No!'

'Into the busy street!' says The Mother, happy at Peg's alarm.

'We all make mistakes,' shrugs The Father. The Mother gives him a look that would sear steak.

'You know what the worst part is?' she says.

'You mean that wasn't the worst part?' gapes the Peg.

'The worst part is that she didn't even *realise he was missing*. He was NINE MONTHS OLD and crawling in the road. Do you know how small a 9-month-old is? There is no way a car would have seen him in time.'

'Heavens,' says the Peg.

The Mother barks a laugh. It's not a nice sound. Mojo twitches in his sleep.

'So what happened?'

'The security patrol car found him. Saw the open garage. Put two and two together. Rang the doorbell.'

'Oh my God,' says the man. 'You were so lucky!'

'Lucky?' splutters The Mother.

'We were,' says The Father. 'Incredibly lucky.'

'What is lucky,' demands The Mother, hot-cheeked again, 'about almost losing my child?'

She stands up with a clatter and begins clearing

away the cream-smeared plates. There is no more talking. I watch her through crescent eyelids. Soiled serviettes roll like tumbleweed into the bin. She sweeps meringue rocks in after them. Tears stream down her face and out of her nose. She swipes at them with her sleeves.

The People get up from the table. They begin rinsing glasses and loading the dishwasher. The Father takes The Mother aside and takes the cutlery out of her hands. Hugs her. He can tell that she is on the verge of some kind of explosion, or deflation. She resists at first, then melts into him. He pats her hair, not unlike the way I pat Mojo. That's what friends do.

I can see that my time has run out. This can't continue. I have to escape tonight. I have no choice. Tonight is the night.

'Thanks for helping,' sniffs The Mother once the kitchen is clean and the tea towels have been hung to dry. She eases the door of the dishwasher closed and turns it on. The water splashes through the machine. The arm whirrs. The soap pocket springs open. She leans against it, as if to keep the door closed. As if, without her weight, it would leap open without warning and douse everyone with foam. Her eyes are black. I don't know why The Father doesn't tell her to wash her panda-eyes off.

'Why don't you sit down, dear,' says the Peg, her pearls hanging freely now. 'We'll make you a nice hot drink. A cup of tea?'

The Mother sags under the sympathy. She sags all the way down onto the couch.

This is good. If they stay in the lounge they won't be able to see me climb out of my cot. I wait until the kettle is boiled and the teaspoons stop tinkling in the mugs and the milk is put away. When I am sure they are all settled in the lounge I use Cuddle Bunny as a step (I have been practising this while The Parents sleep) and climb to the top of the cot and from there I crawl onto the counter. Success! I love being this high up. Getting down, on the other hand, proves to be tricky. Usually I would just jump but I need to be very quiet now.

The People are talking in muted tones. I can no longer make out what they are saying. I hear ceramic mugs being set down on the glass coffee table. I guess that I have five minutes, at the most, before my absence is detected. I'll have longer if The People want to leave and The Parents go out-side to wave. I climb down from the counter onto the floor without making a noise but then my fluffy one-piece pyjama-suit makes me clumsy and I trip over the rippled edge of the oriental carpet and fall spread-eagled onto the floor. Mojo barks.

'Sssh!' I say to Mojo.

The People stop talking. They strain their ears.

'Was that Kade?' asks The Mother, of no one in particular.

'I'm sure he's still fast asleep,' says The Father. 'If he starts crying I'll go to him.'

'Has he always slept in that travel cot? In the dining room?' asks the Peg.

'Yes,' says The Mother. 'I need to have him close-by.'

Ever since I tried to suffocate myself with my baby duvet The Mother monitors my slumber com-pulsively.

'Do you want to check on him now? Will it make you feel better?' asks the man.

'No,' sighs The Mother. 'No, I'm sure he's fine.'

I wait a few seconds and then start making my way to the back door. There is a small step which I almost always forget, but not this time. I hop down into the cold night air. There is still warmth coming from what is left of the fire. The last of the embers glow in the breeze. I scamper across the wide verandah and onto the cold black grass. The ground is uneven and I fall again, but this time it's a soft landing. I crawl the last metre to the pool.

I love the pool. During the day when the sky is in it, it looks like such a happy place. A blue invitation. Now it has swallowed all the night around it. It's an oily abyss.

I crawl to where Mojo has chewed an opening in the pool net. There is no time for goodbyes. I turn around and lever myself in backwards, as if I am scuttling down stairs. In a way, I am. I slip in silently.

People think drowning is a noisy affair. They

imagine shouting and splashing. But when it's a toddler doing the drowning it's as quiet as falling asleep. Once the baby slides underwater you can't hear their flailing. Those are the babies that don't want to escape.

There is no flailing for me. I do not struggle as I sink. Taking the first slug of water is difficult but after that I relax. The water is a lead blanket of calm and my heart begins to drift away. The water tips my chin upwards and lifts my arms, as if inviting me to dance. My body slowly turns and I can feel the darkness is stealing me away: black smoke wrapping itself around my mind, taking me apart.

Fulfilling my destiny is everything I imagined: a soul-searing joy; a terrible bliss. Death is a welcome vacuum. As the last of my thoughts roll away, I think: Finally, I am where I should be.

The darkness is splintered by a cacophony. Urgent barking that goes on and on until there are hurried footsteps and I am hauled rudely out of the water and into the light. Screaming. Shouting. Shaking.

'He's not breathing!' a woman yells. 'I can't find his pulse!'

People are talking urgently. There are strange warm lips on mine. My sleeping lungs balloon. My ribs crack. My bliss evaporates as I cough and choke. I spew water from my mouth. Air assaults my insides. What is happening? Where am I? Who are these People hunched over me with their anxious bulging faces? Why is that creature making such a noise? Is this what it is like to be born? I was happy in the water but this is so cold. So very cold.

The woman who has been pumping my chest cries out when she sees that I am awake. Breathing. She strips the wet fabric from my marble body and puts me under her shirt, directly onto her hot silk of skin. She smells right. She crushes me. She cries. I realise: this must be The Mother. This feels right. There is a man standing: dripping. He stops yelling into his phone and envelops us in his arms. He is The Father. A blanket is thrown around us.

'Kade!' sobs The Mother. 'Kade!' She doesn't have any other words. The Father sobs too.

Kade, I think. That must be my name. That feels right.

I am very tired. I snuggle in, to stop the shivering. I breathe in the milk-silk scent of The Mother. I feel like I am home.

The dog finally stops barking.

∾

THE END

URBAN FANTASY

BLOOD MAGIC SERIES

1. The HighFire Crown
2. The Dream Drinker
3. The Witch Hunter
4. The Ember Isles
5. The Chaos Jar
6. The New Dawn Throne

STANDALONE NOVELS

The Memory of Water

Grey Magic

EverDark

SHORT STORY COLLECTIONS

Sticky Fingers

Sticky Fingers 2

Sticky Fingers 3

Sticky Fingers 4

Sticky Fingers: 36 Deliciously Twisted Short Stories: The
Complete Box Set Collection (Books 1 - 3)

NON-FICTION

The Underachieving Ovary

ABOUT THE AUTHOR

JT Lawrence is a bestselling author and playwright. She lives in Parkview, Johannesburg, in a house with a red front door.

Be notified of giveaways, special deals & new releases
by signing up to JT's mailing list.

www.jt-lawrence.com

ISBN-13: 978-0-9947234-9-9

Published in South Africa by Fire Finch Press

The following stories have been previously published: "Grey
Magic" in *Wax & Wane*, "Bridge Gate" in *Common Thread*. In
addition, "Bridge Gate"; "The Itch"; "The Unsuspecting Gold
Digger"; "Travelling Slacks"; "Something Borrowed"; "She Did
It"; "Pigeon Pair"; "The Little Pink Book"; "Off The Hinge";
"Sticky Fingers" and "Escape" were commissioned, produced
and broadcast by SAFM.

www.jt-lawrence.com
Book design and cover photograph courtesy of Canva.com

❀ Created with Vellum

Made in the USA
Middletown, DE
22 January 2024

48375814R00170